Rock and Run!

Jessica plopped onto her twin sister's blue bedspread and pulled her knees up. "How are we going to get to the Buck's concert next Saturday?"

Elizabeth wasn't very surprised. After all, Jessica almost never took no for an answer. Still, she thought her parents had made their feelings pretty clear. "Jessica," she told her sister, "Mom and Dad aren't punishing us on purpose. They're doing what they think is right, and I, for one, am not about to sneak off behind their backs."

"You can be Miss Goody-Two-Shoes if you want," Jessica announced. "But I'm going to see Johnny Buck in person next week, and no one is going to stop me!"

Bantam-Skylark Books in the SWEET VALLEY TWINS series
Ask your bookseller for the books you have missed

SWEET VALLEY TWINS

Sneaking Out

Written by
Jamie Suzanne

Created by
FRANCINE PASCAL

A BANTAM SKYLARK BOOK®
TORONTO • NEW YORK • LONDON • SYDNEY • AUCKLAND

RL 4, 008–012

SNEAKING OUT

A Bantam Skylark Book / January 1987

Skylark Books is a registered trademark of Bantam Books, Inc.
Registered in U.S. Patent and Trademark Office and elsewhere.

Sweet Valley High and Sweet Valley Twins are trademarks of Francine Pascal.

Conceived by Francine Pascal

Produced by Cloverdale Press Inc.

Cover art by James Mathewuse

ISBN 0-553-15474-5

Published simultaneously in the United States and Canada

Bantam Books are published by Bantam Books, Inc. Its trade-
mark, consisting of the words "Bantam Books" and the por-
trayal of a rooster, is Registered in U.S. Patent and Trademark
Office and in other countries. Marca Registrada. Bantam
Books, Inc., 666 Fifth Avenue, New York, New York 10103.

PRINTED IN THE UNITED STATES OF AMERICA

O   0 9 8 7 6

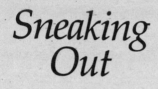

Sneaking
Out

One

◇

"There you are, Lizzie!" Jessica Wakefield left the group of boys and girls standing outside the Sweet Valley Middle School gymnasium and ran toward her twin sister. "I've been waiting here for ages."

Elizabeth studied her sister. Jessica's blue green eyes were larger than ever, and she looked the picture of innocence, from her sunny smile to her sandaled feet.

"Jess, I've been waiting for ages, too," Elizabeth said firmly. "Half an hour to be exact. We decided to meet in *front* of the school, not in back by the gym. Remember?"

When it came to keeping appointments or being on time, Jessica was as different from her identical twin as night from day. Elizabeth never understood how Jessica could think about nothing but having fun all the time. And right now all the fun was centered on cute Bruce Patman and the two slips of paper he was waving high above the heads of the students crowded around him.

"I guess I *did* forget about where we were supposed to meet, Liz," admitted Jessica. "But you'll be glad I did when you hear my news." Her eyes sparkled with excitement.

Elizabeth could never stay mad at her sister for long. Soon she found herself smiling and walking alongside Jessica to join the group gathered around Bruce. "All right," she said with a laugh, "what's the scoop?"

"Boy, ever since you started up the newspaper, you sound just like a reporter," Jessica teased. "OK, news hound, get ready for the most important, spectacular, terrific flash ever! Tickets for the Johnny Buck concert went on sale this morning!"

Johnny Buck! So that was what all the excitement was about. Elizabeth remembered the last time the popular rock star had played in Sweet Valley. Half the kids in town had camped outside the Valley View Hotel, waiting for a glimpse of Johnny. The other half had managed to get tickets to his sellout open-air concert at Sweet Valley's Secca Lake.

Now "The Buck," as his fans called him, was coming back, and the whole school had caught rock fever. Everyone wanted to be part of the crowd that would hear Johnny play songs from his latest album, *The Buck Stops Here.*

Elizabeth watched as Bruce pretended to hand the tickets to Caroline Pearce. Just as Caroline and her friend Elise grabbed for the treasures,

Bruce pulled them away before either girl could touch them. Even if Caroline was the biggest gossip in Sweet Valley Middle School, Elizabeth didn't think Bruce was very funny.

"And those," Elizabeth guessed, "must be two front-row tickets to The Buck's concert."

"You bet they are," squealed Jessica. "Bruce is the first one at school to get tickets. He says the box office is half sold out, even though the show is still a week away!"

Elizabeth frowned. "Bruce Patman *would* be first," she said. "And you can be sure he didn't have to stand in line to get those tickets, either."

Bruce Patman was the only son of the richest family in Sweet Valley and never had to work for anything he wanted. In fact, Caroline had told Elizabeth at lunch that day that Mr. Patman was planning to sponsor two Little League teams just so Bruce could be a pitcher!

"Who cares how he got his tickets?" Jessica tossed her long blond hair impatiently. "The point is, I can finally see Johnny Buck again. Only this time, I'll be watching him sing, instead of looking at him from the street outside a hotel!"

Both girls remembered how thrilled they had been the year before. The handsome young singer had come out of the Valley View Hotel's rear door to sign autographs for the throng of fans who had waited all morning to see him. The crowd had gone wild as Johnny moved closer. Soon everyone was pushing and shoving one another in an effort to touch the singer. Unfortunately, the twins had been forced back into the street.

But the young star had been worth the wait. He looked just like the photographs on his album covers. His curly blond hair fell across his face. Only a few years older than the girls and their friends, he was light-years away in sophistication and maturity.

Johnny Buck had signed only three album jackets before his manager appeared at his side. Whispering into Johnny's ear, the older man began to pull The Buck away from his fans. A huge groan had gone up from the crowd. Hundreds of fans waved record covers, posters, and even their sneakers. They were all begging Johnny to sign just one more souvenir.

That was why, when Johnny Buck suddenly smiled and tossed his striped cap into the crowd, both Elizabeth and Jessica had lunged for the hat as if it were the most valuable thing in the world. When Elizabeth felt her fingers close around the cap's broad brim she thought she was the luckiest girl alive.

A year later, as she stood watching Bruce pulling the tickets from the hands of his Sweet Valley friends, Elizabeth recalled the hurt and confusion she'd felt when Jessica had grabbed the precious hat away.

"Wow!" Jessica had told her sister. "That was close. It's lucky you caught it for me. Those two boys behind us would have ended up with my hat if you hadn't come to the rescue."

"*Your* hat? *I* caught it!"

"Sure. But you saw the way The Buck looked straight at *me* when he threw it. He wanted me to catch it. It's just that when his eyes met mine, I couldn't move. It was the same soft, wonderful feeling I get when I kiss his poster good night. Thank goodness I have a sister who thinks fast!"

So, even though the precious souvenir was rightfully her sister's, Jessica had sulked and pouted until she got her way. Elizabeth had allowed Jessica to keep the cap in her bedroom, beside her stereo. After all, a rock star didn't mean as much to her as her own twin.

"Do you think if I bring my hat, Johnny will autograph it for me?" Jessica was making plans for this year's concert as the twins started home from school.

"You sound as if you already have tickets." Elizabeth laughed. "What makes you think Mom and Dad will even let us go? After all, they said we were too young last year."

"Don't be a silly, Liz. We're in middle school now, and that will make all the difference." Jessica's jaw set. "It's simply *got* to! I've already told Johnny I'm coming."

"You what?!" Elizabeth knew her sister was crazy about Johnny Buck. Who wasn't? But even though her walls were plastered with posters and photos of The Buck, Jessica had never mentioned any conversations with him.

"Well, I didn't actually tell him in person. But I wrote him this long letter that I just know he's going to answer. I told him to look for me right up front after the concert."

"And just what makes you think Johnny Buck is going to pick you out from the biggest crowd in Sweet Valley history?"

"My hat, of course." Jessica was beaming.

"Your hat?"

"I told him I'm the one he threw his cap to at the Valley View, and that I'll be wearing it so he can recognize me at the show. I wrote him about the Unicorns, too, Liz. How the whole club has sworn him eternal devotion and how I want to make him a member."

"You want to make *Johnny Buck* a member of the snob squad?" Elizabeth didn't like many members of the Unicorn Club, an exclusive group of popular girls to which Jessica belonged. And now Elizabeth felt Jessica was carrying her daydreaming too far. Why would a famous rock star want to join a girls' club? Especially when the members spend all their time gossiping about clothes and boys?

"Quiet!" Jessica grabbed Elizabeth's arm, then looked over her shoulder. "It's a secret," she whispered. "I'm going to surprise the girls after Johnny becomes a member. It will be just about the most exciting, fantastic thing any Unicorn ever did for the club!"

"It will also be a miracle." Elizabeth hoped her joking would bring Jessica down to earth, but Jessica talked about Johnny Buck all the way home.

When the two girls walked into the bright, Spanish-tiled kitchen of their family's home, their older brother, Steven, was waiting—with bad news.

"Guess which mature, responsible high school freshman is taking a date to the Johnny Buck concert next weekend?" Steven was lounging against the refrigerator, from which he seemed to have removed everything edible. He began to juggle a package of bologna, a loaf of bread, and a slice of Mrs. Wakefield's orange-walnut coffee cake. Just when it appeared he was about to drop all three, he set everything neatly onto the counter in front of him.

"And," he continued, slapping Jessica's hand too late to prevent her from stealing a walnut from the cake's icing, "guess which two middle schoolers are still too young for The Buck?"

Jessica stopped with the walnut halfway to her open mouth. She could hardly believe what her brother was saying. "What do you mean?" she exclaimed. "It can't be true. Mom and Dad wouldn't do this to us two years in a row!"

Elizabeth stared at her. It didn't look as though Steven was teasing.

Sure enough, their tall brother turned suddenly serious. "I'm sorry, girls," he told them, "I know how badly you wanted to see The Buck this year. That's why I stopped by Dad's office on the way home from school. I thought if I spoke to him first, I could talk him and Mom into going with you. That way I'd be able to buy four more tickets when I picked up tickets for Marcia and me."

Jessica brightened. "Well, I'll admit it's pretty gross to go to a concert with your parents, but it sure beats not going at all! For a minute there, I thought we were going to miss the most exciting event of the year."

"You are," said Steven. "Dad's on a big case out of town that weekend, and Mom's got a meeting with some important clients. Neither of them can make it." Mr. Wakefield was a lawyer, and Mrs. Wakefield worked as an interior designer. Although they made every effort to see that one of them was always home for Steven and the twins, there were times when there just weren't enough parents to go around!

That was what their mother tried to explain to Jessica and Elizabeth when she came home from work a few minutes later. Tall and blond like her daughters, Mrs. Wakefield served as a grade mother for the twins' class and as a member of the high school PTA.

But, she now reminded her children, she also had a promising career. "The plans I designed for the Winthrop Towers have been approved by our board," she told them. "If the client likes them, I'll be responsible for the entire project." Her blue eyes glowed at the prospect. "I'm sorry that the meeting we've had scheduled for over a month conflicts with your big show."

"We are, too, Mom," Elizabeth said sadly. "I really wanted to hear Johnny sing 'Saturday Blues.'"

"It's just not fair," insisted Jessica. "We're so much more mature this year. Ellen Riteman's sister, Debbie, is in Steven's class, and she told Ellen she thought I looked like a freshman."

"Looks are one thing, Jess," Mrs. Wakefield said, smiling, "but maturity is more than skin deep. I love you both, and I don't want my two favorite daughters in over their heads. I'm afraid that's final."

And it was. Mrs. Wakefield remained firm,

even though Jessica put on one of her longest, saddest crying scenes, and Elizabeth promised they would get a ride straight home.

Mr. Wakefield remained firm too. The minute he stepped inside the door, he found Jessica hanging on his arm, a tearful expression on her face.

"Oh, Dad," she wailed piteously, "you simply *have* to let us go see The Buck. If you don't, Elizabeth and I will just *die!*"

Jessica stopped crying and studied her father to see if she'd gotten through. His smile looked as warm as ever, but Jessica could tell he wasn't giving in.

"You won't die," he assured Jessica. "But, with more performances like this one, you might have a future in the theater!"

But Jessica was far from finished. As soon as the Wakefields sat down to dinner, she continued her campaign. She spent more time sniffling than eating. Just before dessert, she played her most dramatic scene of all. She wiped her eyes with a napkin, sat up very tall, and spoke in a calm, even voice.

"I'm sorry, Mom and Dad. Elizabeth and I are being totally unfair. After all, we can't expect you to give up your lives just because we want to go to a silly rock concert."

Everyone at the table seemed surprised by her sudden change of heart. Now that she had their attention, Jessica really poured it on. "Those tickets cost twenty-five dollars apiece, and two extras would be a big expense. We'll go with Steven and Marcia. We'll be really good. They won't even know we're along. And we'll even work to pay our own way!"

"You bet!" chimed in Elizabeth, surprised by her twin's determination. "We can mow lawns and run errands. And there are lots of young children in the neighborhood. We could even baby-sit!"

Mrs. Wakefield reached for her husband's hand, then smiled at the girls. "I think you've overlooked Steven in all this," she said. Steven's face reddened as she tousled his dark hair affectionately. "This is his first date with Marcia Crane. I think he's nervous enough without being saddled with you two mischievous kids!"

"That's right," Mr. Wakefield added, a patient firmness in his tone. "You know that your mother and I don't enjoy disappointing you two. And you know it isn't simply a question of money. We'd be glad to help you get tickets if there were any way we could go along, too. But there's not, and we are not going to take the easy way out of this problem by giving in and letting you fight a crowd that's too old and too fast for you. And that, young ladies, is my final word on the matter. Case dismissed."

Because Mr. Wakefield was a lawyer, that comment often made his daughters laugh. But no one at the Wakefield dinner table laughed that night. In fact, after the twins had done the dishes they hid away in their upstairs bedrooms. Neither girl found anything about the horrible day the least bit amusing!

But Elizabeth couldn't keep a black mood for long. Alone in the cheerful cream-and-blue bedroom she'd decorated herself, she soon regained her usual optimism. She decided that the only thing to do was to work hard to earn her parents' trust so that next year things would be different. Within a few minutes, she had forgotten all about Johnny Buck and was trying to remember how to convert fractions to decimals. That was when the bathroom door that connected her room to Jessica's suddenly flew open.

"I can't think," Jessica announced, exploding like a blond bomb in the middle of Elizabeth's homework. "I think I need advice from someone who got a four-minute head start in the world!"

The two always joked about the fact that Elizabeth was four minutes older than Jessica. Sometimes Elizabeth really *felt* like a big sister to her headstrong twin. "OK, Jess," she said, closing her math book. "What's the problem?"

"The same problem we've had all day, of course!" Jessica plopped onto her sister's blue corduroy bedspread and pulled her knees up. "How are we going to get to The Buck's concert next Saturday?"

Elizabeth wasn't surprised. After all, Jessica almost never took no for an answer. Still, she thought her parents had made their feelings clear. "Jessica," she said, "Mom and Dad aren't punishing us. They're doing what they think is right, and I, for one, am not about to sneak off behind their backs.

"Besides," she continued, "you don't have twenty-five *cents*, not to mention twenty-five dollars, to spend on a ticket. You just paid a fortune for that new blouse from Kendall's."

Jessica crinkled her nose with distaste. "That

old thing! It's too hideous for words. I don't know why I ever saved up three weeks' allowance to buy it. I'm going to take it right back tomorrow!"

"You can't, Jess. It was on sale. Why don't you face facts? We're just going to have to wait until next year."

"Next year!" Jessica looked as horrified as if her twin had suggested waiting until her next lifetime. "I sure came to the wrong person for advice!" She lifted herself from her sister's bed and opened the door to the bathroom. "You can be Miss Goody-Two-Shoes if you want," she announced, determined, "but *I'm* going to see Johnny Buck in person next week, and nobody is going to stop me!"

Two

◇

"I figure," Elizabeth told her twin as they walked to school several days later, "that you called every house in Sweet Valley this weekend." She spoke in a deep, gruff voice, imitating their father's best courtroom manner. "You proved beyond a shadow of a doubt that no one in town needs their children watched, their grass cut, or their car waxed."

Jessica was not at all amused by her sister's joke. "I never should have bought that blouse at Kendall's." She stopped in the middle of the sidewalk and studied Elizabeth as if she were seeing her for the very first time. "The color is all wrong for *me*. But it would be just dynamite on *you*."

Elizabeth couldn't help laughing out loud at her sister's transparent plan. "Jessica Wakefield, if you think you can talk me into buying that blouse from you so you can sneak off to see The Buck, you're crazy!" But Jessica didn't know when to give up trying to get what she wanted, especially when it was something as vital as a Johnny Buck concert.

"Well, you always *did* look better in purple. Besides, the way you've been hoarding your allowance lately, I bet you've saved about a trillion dollars."

It was true, Elizabeth *had* been saving up her allowance and even her lunch money. But *not* to buy a purple blouse from Jessica. Aside from that, purple was Elizabeth's most unfavorite color. But most of all, Elizabeth didn't want any of her classmates making the gross mistake of thinking that she was a Unicorn!

"Jess, we're already ten minutes late because you couldn't decide how to wear your hair today. Don't be a pest about how fabulous I look in purple. I won't have a penny to spare this week if I'm going to buy those earrings for Mom's birthday."

Jessica had been with Elizabeth when she found the gold hoop earrings at the Valley Mall. Their mother loved oversize earrings, and these would make a perfect gift. But Mrs. Wakefield's birthday was still a whole month off. The concert was just four days away! If only Jessica could think of a way to postpone buying her mother's birthday present, then she could borrow the money she needed from Elizabeth.

Even after the twins had raced through the hallways of Sweet Valley Middle School, Jessica was still scheming. As the first bell rang, they rushed to put their books and jackets into their lockers, and then Elizabeth dashed off toward homeroom.

But Jessica had more important things to worry about than school bells. Finally, as the last bell rang, she gave herself a quick inspection in the tiny mirror she kept in her locker. Her hair looked all wrong, so she decided to put it up into a bun like a ballet dancer's when she saw the solution to her problem walking down the hall.

"Amy Sutton! I'm simply dying to talk to you. Where have you been hiding?" Jessica charged up to the tall girl with stringy blond hair, who'd stopped a few lockers away.

Balancing her books on one knee while she struggled with her combination lock, Amy looked at Jessica with startled blue eyes. She and Elizabeth were good friends, but Amy was not at all the sort of girl that Jessica sought out. Amy was too much of a tomboy for Jessica.

"What's up, Jessica?" Amy succeeded in opening her locker and tumbling her books into the bottom so she could wriggle out of her denim jacket. "Is there a Booster practice after school today?" Agile and athletic, Amy had recently made the Booster Club, a middle-school cheering squad organized by some of the Unicorns.

"Well, there *is* a practice." Jessica giggled and put her arm around Amy. "But it's not at school." Standing next to Elizabeth's friend, Jessica realized triumphantly that she and Amy were practically the same height. It looked as if her troubles were over. "I thought maybe you and I could go over some of the cheers at my house."

Amy picked up the binder she needed for her first-period class and slammed her locker shut. "You mean you want me to come home with you?" She couldn't help letting the surprise show in her voice. After all, Jessica had been furious with Amy for trying out for the cheering squad. Even though Amy was the best baton twirler on the squad, she had a feeling that Jessica still resented her.

"Sure. Why not?" Jessica's smile seemed sweet and genuine. "We Boosters have to stick together!"

Amy had always been at a loss for words around Jessica. But now, as Elizabeth's dynamic twin chattered and giggled, Amy began to feel that Jessica Wakefield actually liked her. Even though they were totally different, maybe they could be friends.

And that was exactly what Amy told Elizabeth at lunch. "Just think," she announced with shy pride, "there will be three of us walking home from school together. Won't it be fun?"

Elizabeth was surprised and delighted that her twin had at last seen how wonderful Amy was. She remembered all the times Jessica had dismissed Amy and couldn't help wondering now about the sudden switch.

"That's wonderful," she told her best friend. "But we'll have to make it a threesome next time. Mr. Bowman says the English office won't be free until after school, so I'll have to wait until then to run off the newspaper. Tell Jess I'll meet you two at the house as soon as I can."

The photocopying seemed to take forever that afternoon. Mr. Bowman's coffee spilled on the entire pile of page twos, and Elizabeth's stapler tore the pages instead of fastening them. It was well after four-thirty before a stack of two hundred copies of *The Sweet Valley Sixers* was ready for distribution, and Elizabeth started home.

When Elizabeth opened the door to the Wakefields' handsome split-level ranch, she heard shrill laughter coming from Jessica's upstairs bedroom. Elizabeth rushed upstairs and into her sister's room. She was shocked to find Amy standing in front of the full-length mirror, wearing the purple blouse Jessica had bought at Kendall's. It was a few sizes too big for her.

"Doesn't it look stunning?" cooed Jessica. She was sitting on her pink bedspread, looking at Amy as if she were wearing a designer prom dress. "I mean it's simply *made* for you, Amy. It's totally you."

Amy caught Elizabeth's reflection in the mirror. She turned to face her best friend, the neckline of the purple blouse nearly falling off one thin shoulder. "It seems a little big to me," she offered shyly. "What do you think, Liz?"

Elizabeth hoped her face didn't tell Amy what she thought. Because what she thought was that her sister was so anxious to see Johnny Buck that she didn't care whom she took advantage of. It made her angry and ashamed to see poor Amy swimming in Jessica's blouse.

"It's all set, Lizzie," purred Jessica, joining them in front of the mirror. "Amy's buying my blouse. She looks terrific. Doesn't she?"

Even though she was furious at Jessica, Elizabeth loved her twin too much to expose her nasty plot in front of Amy. But she wasn't about to let her trusting friend wear that purple tent to school!

"I think you're right, Amy," she said slowly. "It is a little large on you. But I'll bet that sale is still on at Kendall's. I'm sure you could get that blouse in your size, even if it has to be a different color." She looked straight at Jessica and put her arm around Amy. "Just because the Unicorns are all color-blind, it doesn't mean the rest of us have to be."

Amy studied herself in the mirror again. She had to admit that the blouse was much too big, even if Jessica's praise had made her feel gorgeous. "I still think it's pretty," she told both twins. "So pretty that I'm going right down to Kendall's after school tomorrow and find one in my size. Why don't all three of us go?"

"Uh—I don't think I can." Jessica looked away quickly. "The Unicorns are meeting at the Dairi Burger. Besides," she added, giving her sister a wounded look, "I'm going to be busy thinking up ways to make lots of money *F A S T.*"

Jessica continued to look wounded long after Amy had left. Throughout dinner, her tragic expression and angry silence would have convinced anyone that it was Elizabeth, not Jessica, who had tried to take advantage of Amy.

"I hope you're satisfied," she wailed as the twins loaded the dishwasher. "Now everything's ruined and I'll never get to see Johnny."

Elizabeth plunged her hands into the soapy water and scrubbed a muffin tin extra hard to keep from exploding. "There are other ways to make money," she told Jessica, "without tricking it away

from someone." Elizabeth couldn't believe that
Jessica had almost let Amy make a fool of herself
just to get what she wanted. Elizabeth was as embarrassed as her twin should have been.

Suddenly Jessica stopped pouting. She
turned and faced Elizabeth. "You're right, big sister," she said in her best making-up voice. She
hated it when Elizabeth got mad at her. After all,
Unicorns or no Unicorns, her twin was her very
best friend on earth. "Let's call a truce, Lizzie. I
won't hold any more clothes sales if you'll stop
thinking I'm so awful."

Elizabeth burst out laughing. "It's a deal, little
sister. Why don't we seal the bargain with shakes
at Casey's Place?"

The twins loved the old-fashioned ice-cream
parlor with its round marble tables. The list of fla-
vors went from one end of the counter all the way
to the other. It didn't take much pleading to convince Mr. and Mrs. Wakefield and Steven that the
whole family needed an ice-cream break. Everyone piled into the Wakefields' maroon van and
headed downtown for the Valley Mall. Casey's was
as crowded as always, so the twins volunteered to
stand in line. The others found the only empty
table in sight. Soon Steven relayed his parents'
orders for two butterscotch sundaes with chopped
nuts. Jessica and Elizabeth didn't need to ask what
their brother wanted. He always ordered the
Casey Special: four scoops of ice cream on a walnut brownie with whipped cream, chocolate
syrup, cookie crumble, and a maraschino cherry.

As the long line of customers inched forward,

Jessica began to glance around the room absently for something to take her mind off waiting. She noticed a bulletin board hanging to her right and studied the jumble of notices and flyers pinned up on it.

There were a few messages about cars for sale. Several notes were from people offering piano lessons in their homes. Every note pinned to the board, Jessica realized wistfully, had been written by someone trying to earn money. Maybe if she had thought to put up a message of her own a week ago, she could have earned her ticket to see Johnny Buck. Now there was no hope left at all.

Then her eye caught a sign that stood out from all the others. It was written on blue notepaper in very neat, elegant handwriting. As soon as Jessica realized what the note said, she tore the card off the bulletin board.

"That's it! That's it!" she squealed, jumping up and down in the middle of the long line, nearly stumbling into the arms of a woman behind her. "Liz, I forgive you completely. Everything's going to be fine. In fact, everything's going to be just perfect!"

Elizabeth felt happy to see her sister so excited, even without knowing why. Jessica's enthusiasm was always contagious. "What is it, Jess?" she asked. "What's written on that piece of paper?"

Jessica folded the blue notepaper carefully and slipped it into the pocket of her jeans. "Oh, nothing," she said, sounding mysterious. "Just the answer to my prayers. That's all."

Three

◇

As soon as the Wakefields arrived home from Casey's, Elizabeth and Steven groaned and buckled down to their homework. But Jessica could think only about the exciting discovery she had made on the bulletin board at the ice cream parlor.

"Liz," she called softly, opening the bathroom door to her twin's room. "Can you take your nose out of those boring books long enough to help me with something?"

Elizabeth looked up from her desk to find her sister smiling the smug grin that signaled a plot was hatching. She couldn't help smiling back. "So you've decided to tell me about that mysterious blue paper after all."

"You know I can never keep secrets from you. Besides, I need someone to stand guard duty while I make a super-urgent phone call." Popping with pride at her cleverness, Jessica pulled the notice from her pocket and unfolded it on Elizabeth's desk.

A headline was written along the top of the paper. "Animal Lover," it said in neat, graceful script. Underneath were the words on which Jessica was pinning all her hopes:

Needed for three days:
Dog-sitter to provide
loving, tender care for
well-behaved pet. $25
Call C. Bramble
555-9721

"But, Jess," Elizabeth protested as soon as she'd read the ad, "you *hate* dogs. That time the Hendersons came to Dad's barbecue with their Chihuahua, I thought you were going to jump out of your skin."

It was true. For as long as she could remember, Jessica had detested the sight, smell, and touch of all dogs. In fact, although she wouldn't admit it even to herself, she was deathly afraid of them. And, somehow, they always knew it.

"I *do* wish it could have been another kind of pet," she confided now. "A nice quiet cat, or a goldfish. Even a parakeet wouldn't be so bad. Anything that wouldn't insist on putting its filthy paws in your lap and slobbering all over you with its disgusting tongue."

To Jessica, Johnny Buck was worth any sacrifice. There was just no other way to earn money in the few days remaining until Saturday. Picturing The Buck's handsome face leaning close to hers while he autographed his cap, Jessica grabbed

Elizabeth's hand and pulled her twin into the hall toward the phone. While Elizabeth watched to make certain no one in the family interrupted, Jessica dialed the number on the notice.

C. Bramble turned out to be Catherine Bramble, an elderly-sounding woman who lived nearby in a small home on Shady Dale Court. She told Jessica that the job was still available and that after school the next day would be an excellent time to visit and discuss the details.

Jessica hung up the phone, beaming triumphantly. She hugged Elizabeth and did three pirouettes down the length of the hall. "I did it! Just think, by this time tomorrow I'll be twenty-five dollars richer and a billion times happier!" But suddenly, her sunny mood dimmed. "*If* I get this job, that is. Oh, Lizzie, how will I ever get through that interview? You've got to come with me. You always know what to say!"

"Jess," Elizabeth reminded her twin, "this is all your idea. I don't want any part of it."

"But, Liz, what if the dog is there? What if Mrs. Bramble expects me to actually touch it? I'll die. I'll simply die. I told her I'd go over right after school tomorrow. It would only take a minute or two, and you know what a big fuss little old ladies and animals always make over you. You'll make just the right impression. I know you will."

"Right after school tomorrow, in case you've forgotten, we have dance class with Madame André. You were her star pupil until you made the Booster Club. Now you've decided cheerleading is more important than ballet. And if you miss one more lesson, I have a feeling those veins in her forehead are going to explode!"

Both twins giggled at the thought of their dignified dance teacher losing control. "All right. You win," said Jessica. "I'll go to the interview by myself if you make things right with Madame André. Tell her I'm in bed with pneumonia, begging to dance. Tell her I broke both legs, but I'll be in next week. Or tell her I drowned in the ocean with my toes pointed all the way down." Jessica clutched at her throat and fell heavily to the floor.

"I'm sorry, Madame André," Elizabeth announced in a mock-solemn voice. "My sister won't be joining us today. But I'm proud to tell you that her last words were, 'Shoulders back. Stomach in.'"

Just then Steven opened the door. He found his sisters collapsed in a hysterical heap, laughing so hard they had tears in their eyes. "You two," he said, "are definitely weird."

Steven didn't change his opinion the next morning at breakfast, when he overheard Elizabeth giving Jessica some last-minute instructions. "Just remember," he heard her say, "hold your hand out so he can lick it before you try to scratch his ears."

"I always thought *you* were the sensible one," Steven told Elizabeth as he scooped up his books from the sideboard and headed for the front door. "But if you think that's any way to get a boyfriend, I'm glad *I'm* not in sixth grade."

Elizabeth laughed out loud as the door slammed and Steven disappeared. But Jessica was too worried even to smile. All the way to school, she thought anxiously about her interview with Mrs. Bramble. At lunch that day, she didn't even joke about how many meatballs plump Lois Waller had put on her spaghetti. Instead, she sat quietly, listening intently to her twin's advice on the care and feeding of dogs. By the time three-thirty came and she was actually standing outside the door of 132 Shady Dale Court, Jessica was a nervous wreck.

It was a relief to find that Mrs. Bramble was a friendly woman. Her gentle smile had a way of making Jessica feel at home right away. Best of all, Jessica noted as she took a seat on the blue flowered sofa, there wasn't a dog in sight. From the neatly carpeted living room to the open kitchen and bedroom, she didn't spot so much as a discarded bone or a single dog toy.

Relaxing, Jessica sank into the plump sofa and half-listened as Mrs. Bramble described her trip. She'd planned to visit her family south of San Francisco. She'd be gone only a few days, she told Jessica, and would be back on Saturday.

Johnny Buck's concert was Saturday afternoon. Jessica was afraid for a minute that the job wouldn't allow her to see The Buck after all. But once Mrs. Bramble explained that she would be home before lunch, there was no turning off the Wakefield charm. Within minutes, Mrs. Bramble decided that she had never met anyone as fond of dogs as her young visitor. Jessica became lively and animated, chatting about the countless dogs in her life.

"And," she assured her prospective employer, "my whole family loves dogs as much as I do. I just know that if I brought your dog home, all of us would be fighting over who got to take care of it."

"My dear, that's so wonderful to hear." Mrs. Bramble was smiling with delight. "That's just what we'll do then."

Jessica, who was about to list all the animal charities to which her parents contributed, stopped in midsentence. "We will?"

"Of course. It's a fine idea. Quite frankly, I hadn't planned on giving this job to a schoolchild. My Sally needs a lot of attention during the daytime, so I intended to ask someone to stay here in my house with her." Mrs. Bramble looked at Jessica as if the matter were already decided. "But since you're so fond of dogs and since your family feels the same way, I guess Sally will just move in with you for a few days. Now, you're sure your mother won't mind?"

Jessica wasn't sure at all. In fact, she remembered only too well the time their neighbor's poodle ate the begonias out of all the planters around their pool. Mrs. Wakefield hadn't sounded like a dog lover at all when she sent the culprit howling back to his own backyard!

"Mind? Why, of course not." Jessica sounded much less confident than before. "Everyone will certainly be surprised."

You bet they will, she added grimly to herself. How was she ever going to explain *this* to her parents?

"Then, it's all settled. You can pick up Sally tomorrow night, because my bus leaves first thing Thursday morning. Isn't that wonderful news, Sally? You're going on vacation too."

Jessica suddenly swallowed the cookie Mrs. Bramble had given her, without chewing it. Was the woman's dog an imaginary pet? Jessica looked around the room again, but still she saw no sign of a dog.

"Come on, dear," coaxed Mrs. Bramble. "Come and meet your new friend." The little woman clapped her hands, and Jessica leaped from her seat. The oldest, fattest cocker spaniel she had ever seen crawled sleepily from underneath the sofa.

"Sally, this is Jessica. Jessica, this is Sally," said Mrs. Bramble, looking very pleased with both of them.

Jessica stood rooted to the spot, staring into Sally's teary brown eyes. She shuddered to think that this horrible old beast had been snoozing just underneath her feet while she'd been talking with Mrs. Bramble! Sally, mildly interested in the new visitor, walked slowly toward Jessica. She looked very much like an oversize dust mop swaying across the floor. Jessica held her breath and dropped to her knees beside the dog.

"Hello, Sally." She forced herself to hold out her hand the way Elizabeth had taught her. She shut her eyes tight as the old dog licked it with her tongue. "She looks just like I pictured her," she told Mrs. Bramble.

"She's my old darling." The woman beamed

at Sally, who now began to dig her sharp claws into Jessica's newest pair of jeans while she licked Jessica's face as thoroughly as if she were washing it. "Sally and I have been together ever since she was a tiny, frisky puppy."

Jessica nodded and smiled, summoning all her willpower to keep from pushing the lumpy dog from her lap. She wasn't sure how, but she managed to sit with Sally for another ten minutes while Mrs. Bramble recited an endless list of instructions. Sally, it seemed, ate only soft dog food because she had very few teeth left. She needed to be fed and walked twice a day.

"Please, my dear," Mrs. Bramble begged Jessica, "take good care of my precious." The elderly woman's eyes misted over as if she were going to cry. "I don't know what I'd do without her."

Jessica, who had hardly heard a word, assured Mrs. Bramble that her dear pet would be in the best of hands. The dog would be fed and stroked and spoiled. And yes, of course, hugged at least three times a day.

"Very well. I'll give you some money now for Sally's food, and I'll pay you twenty-five dollars on Saturday when I pick her up." Mrs. Bramble lifted the heavy dog from Jessica's knees and placed her tenderly on her own lap.

Jessica had forgotten that work was usually paid for after it is completed. But she knew that she couldn't count on getting a ticket to The Buck's show if she waited until Saturday to buy it. Desperate, she tried to think of a way to convince Mrs. Bramble to pay her in advance.

"I wonder," Jessica ventured timidly. "I mean, it would be so wonderful if I could have the money now. Saturday will be too late."

"Too late for what, dear?" Mrs. Bramble stopped stroking Sally's shaggy neck to look at Jessica, who now had a timid expression on her face.

"You see, my sister and I have been saving all our money," explained Jessica slowly. "My mother's birthday is coming, and we want to buy her something extra special. That's why I applied for this job, aside from the fact that I adore dogs, that is."

"And her birthday's before Saturday, is it? I see. Well, in that case, I think Sally and I can pay you right now. Can't we, Sally, dear?" Mrs. Bramble slipped the fat dog off her lap and walked to the closet. She found her purse and took out two ten-dollar bills and one five. When she placed the money in Jessica's hand, she was rewarded with a dazzling smile that showed the dimple on Jessica's left cheek.

Jessica ran home with the money safely in her pocket. She felt only the teensiest bit guilty about the way Mrs. Bramble had stood by her door to wave goodbye. "Don't forget," the old woman had reminded Jessica as she left, "to tell your mother happy birthday from Sally and me!"

Four

◇

When the twins arrived at school the next morning, the members of the Unicorn Club were standing in a small group just outside the main
entrance. As soon as she saw her friends, Jessica
waved a hurried goodbye to her sister and rushed
to join them. Lila Fowler and Ellen Riteman, her
two sixth-grade pals, turned to greet her. The
older members were too busy listening to Janet
Howell to look up.

"He's a junior and he lives in San Francisco.
He's coming down for the weekend because he's
never missed a Johnny Buck concert." Janet, who
was the eighth-grade president of the Unicorns,
didn't sound at all like her usual bossy self. Her
voice was all bubbly and excited, and her words
tumbled out so fast Jessica could hardly keep up.

"*Nice!*" Lila exclaimed. She then turned to Jessica and said, "I suppose you're going to tell us
you're traveling to the show in Johnny Buck's pri-
vate jet?"

"Not exactly." Jessica waited until she had the whole group's attention. When all the girls were listening, she lowered her long lashes and added quietly, "I'm meeting Johnny after the show."

Lila's pretty face registered amazement. "You're *what*?" she shrieked. The Unicorns gathered in a tight circle around Jessica, all of them dying to hear more.

Everyone, including Janet, seemed to have forgotten about her brother's roommate. "You mean," Janet asked eagerly, "you've actually talked to Johnny Buck in person?"

"Johnny's eyes did all his talking for him," answered Jessica dreamily. "Last year, he picked me out of a whole crowd to throw his hat to."

"Oh, *that* old story again." Janet seemed relieved that Jessica's news was disappointing. "We've all heard how you got The Buck's cap a million times. Let's not make it a million and one!"

But Jessica wasn't finished. She paused dramatically, then stared at Janet with wide eyes. "Oh, then I guess you don't want to hear about The Buck becoming an honorary Unicorn."

Even Janet was stunned into silence. For several seconds, all the girls stood frozen around Jessica. Then, suddenly, everyone started talking at once.

"It's just too wonderful!" cooed Mary Giaccio, a seventh-grader.

"I can't believe it!" gasped Tamara Chase, another older Unicorn. "The Buck joining the Unicorns?"

Kimberly Haver's dark eyes flashed. "Tell us

everything, Jessica. Absolutely every single wonderful detail!"

"Just a minute." Janet looked suspicious and hopeful at once. "Who says that just because Johnny Buck tossed Jessica a hat, he's all of a sudden going to join our club?"

"Oh, he already knows all about us, Janet. I wrote him all about the Unicorns. I even wrote my last letter to him in purple." Even though Jessica's "last" letter to the star had also been her first, she was certain everything would work out as she dreamed, if only she could get to the concert on Saturday.

"So *this* year," she announced grandly, "I'm not going to have the same old story to tell. In fact, I'm meeting The Buck after his show, and I'm getting my hat decorated with the most special autograph in all the world!"

"How incredibly romantic." Ellen sighed.

"So he really *is* going to meet you?" asked Janet. The Unicorn's president was looking at Jessica with new respect.

"Yes, unless—" Jessica fluttered her lashes again like the heroine of a teenage soap opera. "Unless my parents stop us. You see, my mom and dad don't want me to see him."

"How utterly tragic!" Ellen gasped. "I wish I could help you, Jess, but my parents won't let me go to the show."

"Mine, either," admitted Mary.

"Nor mine," added Tamara. "They say rock concerts can get too wild."

Jessica was surprised that the Wakefields

weren't the only parents in town who had decided that the concert was off limits this Saturday. A week ago, she'd been convinced that she and Elizabeth would be the only kids in Sweet Valley to miss the show.

"Of course, I'd offer you a ride," said Janet, sounding too sweet to be true. "But my brother says his roommate drives a tiny little car, so I'm afraid there just won't be any extra room."

"That's OK," Lila announced, coming to her friend's rescue. "Jessica can go with me." Everyone knew that Lila's father was much too busy building and setting up new plants to care what his spoiled daughter did with her time. "I'm sure your parents would let you sleep over at my house on Saturday, Jess. You don't even have to mention the concert."

Jessica was thrilled. It was a perfect plan. The fact that it had to be kept secret made it even more exciting. "Lila Fowler," she told her friend, "you are completely brilliant, and you'd better bring all your Buck albums with you to the show. I'm going to ask Johnny to sign every one of them!"

When the first bell rang, the Unicorns were still sighing over Jessica's daring romance. Before the second bell, each girl made a solemn promise not to tell anyone about Lila's plot to help Jessica sneak out to the concert. As Lila and Jessica raced up the stairs to the school's central corridor, they made plans to meet after school to buy their concert tickets.

All through English, Elizabeth noticed her twin's wide smile. She thought it was strange that

Jessica looked so happy, especially when the class was reviewing sentence diagrams. It was a subject that Jessica hated. But Jessica was the very picture of contentment. And when Mr. Bowman called on her and it became obvious that she hadn't the least idea what a prepositional phrase was, she continued to wear the same dreamy grin.

Even lunch couldn't destroy Jessica's romantic mood. The fact that the cafeteria was serving everyone's all-time least-favorite meal—creamed beef with scalloped potatoes—didn't seem to make any difference to her at all. Elizabeth was puzzled as she watched her twin devour the soupy beef with relish.

"Jess, you're usually the pickiest eater on earth. How come you're the only person in this whole room enjoying the Sweet Valley mystery meat?"

The twins grinned at each other. Jessica couldn't wait any longer to let Elizabeth in on her terrific secret.

"I could eat dog-food mud pies today," she declared happily. "And they would still taste great. Lila and I are buying our tickets to The Buck's concert after school today." She saw the worried look cross her sister's face. "Best of all, I don't even have to lie to Mom and Dad. I'm sleeping over at Lila's on Saturday. It's all set."

Elizabeth knew very well what that meant. It meant that their parents would try to make up for Jessica's missing the big concert by agreeing to let her spend the night with her friend. It also meant that Jessica could sneak off with Lila to Secca

Lake. It meant that, as always, Jessica would get what she wanted.

Elizabeth knew she should be angry at this latest scheme, but looking at Jessica's sunny smile was enough to stop Elizabeth from lecturing her twin. It was hard not to admire Jessica's determination, although she herself would never go against her parents' wishes.

"Of course, you've got to promise never to tell Mom and Dad, Lizzie." Jessica leaned across the table and dropped her cup of butterscotch pudding onto her sister's lunch tray. "I'll give you my desserts for the rest of my life if you'll do this special favor for me. I won't ask you to do my math homework ever again. I'll do the dishes *and* clear the table from now on!"

Elizabeth knew how short Jessica's memory could be when it came to promises. Still, she loved her impetuous twin more than any other person in the world.

"OK, OK." She laughed, returning the pudding to Jessica's tray. "I don't need to be bribed, especially with *butterscotch*. The next time you want me to keep a secret, you'd better choose a day when they're serving chocolate!"

When school was over and Jessica and Lila had bought their tickets, only one problem remained. How was Jessica going to persuade her mother to let her keep Sally for the next three days? As she walked home from the ticket outlet in town, Jessica remembered the interview with Mrs. Bramble and the awful, hairy price she would have to pay to see her idol.

"Guess what?" she asked Steven and her mother when she found them in the backyard. Steven, dressed in blue tennis shorts and sneakers, was skimming the pool. Mrs. Wakefield was busy painting the low white brick wall that curved around the huge bed of flowers she had planted last fall. The bright southern California sun poured over the large, grassy lawn and bathed everything in an afternoon glow.

"I met the dearest little old lady who lives practically around the corner."

"That's nice, dear." Mrs. Wakefield continued painting in smooth, even strokes.

"She has this cute old dog that she can't bear to put in a kennel."

Steven looked up. This was the first time he had ever heard his sister mention a dog without sounding as if she were talking about a flesh-eating monster. "Why would she have to put her dog in a kennel?" he asked.

"Because she wants to visit her family outside of San Francisco. She and Sally—that's her dog—have been together ever since Sally was a tiny puppy. They've never been separated, and Mrs. Bramble doesn't know what to do."

"That's a shame," sympathized Mrs. Wakefield, still brushing carefully over the wall.

"It sure is," Jessica answered with conviction. "I just wish there were some way to help. Sally is absolutely no trouble. I mean all she does is eat and sleep. You know how it is when you get old."

Mrs. Wakefield smiled. "Not quite yet," she said, turning away from her painting. "Knowing how you've always felt about dogs, young lady, I'd say this Mrs. Bramble must be quite a wonderful person to make you so concerned."

"Oh, she definitely is, Mom. She's terrific, and she'll only be gone for three days. I told her I was sure you wouldn't mind. I said I'd walk Sally every morning and every night."

"*What?*" Steven couldn't believe his ears. "You actually volunteered to take care of a dog?"

"Well," Jessica answered quietly, "Mrs. Bramble insists on paying me. But I really just want to give her some peace of mind about her sweet old pet."

"I'm not sure I understand," interrupted Mrs. Wakefield. "Do you mean to say that you've contracted to get up early for three mornings to walk a dog? Jessica, you are always the last one in the family to come down for breakfast in the morning."

"I know that, Mom. But I promised Mrs. Bramble I'd walk Sally at least twice a day." Jessica's eyelashes began to flutter, and her voice got very soft. "The only trouble is that Mrs. Bramble wants Sally to stay with us."

"With us!" Mrs. Wakefield put her paintbrush down and walked over to stand beside her daughter. "Jessica, I am proud you want to help a neighbor. I do think you should have consulted your father and me before you offered our home, though."

"Oh, Mommy," answered Jessica, her huge aqua eyes brimming with tears. "It's just that she had nowhere else to turn. Sally is used to attention all day long, and she'd positively pine away if she were left alone in that empty house all day." Jessica looked as frightened as if it were *she* who might be left alone. "And you know a kennel would be even worse. Think of her locked in some tiny, smelly cage. Oh, please. Please. It's only for three days."

The last thing Mrs. Wakefield wanted to discourage in her daughter was loving concern. She was touched by the kindness Jessica had shown Mrs. Bramble. Although she had not forgotten her encounter with the begonia-eating poodle, she decided that Jessica's generosity should be matched by her family's.

"All right, Jess. I suppose that if you can overcome your fear of dogs for three days, the rest of us can roll up our sleeves and help you. Right, Steven?"

"I guess so," answered Steven, still puzzled by his sister's display of neighborliness. "Let me just get this straight, Jess. Are you sure this animal has hair, four legs, and a tail?"

"Of course, silly. She even sat on my lap," replied Jessica.

"That does it," exclaimed Steven. "I think the real Jessica's been replaced with an incredible look-alike!"

"Laugh if you want to," Jessica told him, treating her brother to a radiant smile. "That little dog means an awful lot to me. I intend to take very, very good care of her."

Five

◇

Mr. Wakefield was as impressed with Jessica's good intentions as his wife and son had been. In fact, it was no time at all before they were praising generous Jessica to the skies. They all offered to help her in any way they could. Her dog-sitting job became a Wakefield project. Sally's arrival was eagerly awaited by the entire family.

Later that night, when Mrs. Bramble called, Jessica convinced Elizabeth to go with her to pick up the dog. Mrs. Bramble and Sally were eagerly awaiting the twins' arrival. A huge dog bed full of blankets, toys, and treats was already stacked up by the door. Mrs. Bramble was bubbling over with enthusiasm and gratitude when they finally arrived.

"Why, my goodness, I thought I was leaving Sally with just *one* perfect pet-sitter. Now, it appears I have two—and I can't tell who's who!" She clapped her hands with delight, looking from one girl to the other.

"This is my twin sister, Elizabeth," Jessica explained. "This is Mrs. Bramble."

"I'm very pleased to meet you." Elizabeth shook Mrs. Bramble's hand and, smiling, patted the dog on the head. "And Sally, too."

"I can't tell you what a relief it is," Mrs. Bramble told Elizabeth, "to know your sister will be watching my dear Sally." As she talked she piled the dog bed and goodies into Elizabeth's arms. "I can't think of anyone who could give her more love."

Elizabeth, wondering how her dog-shy twin had managed even to stay in the same room with Sally, nodded and asked if there was a number where Mrs. Bramble could be reached.

The kind woman wrote her family's address and phone number on a piece of paper and slipped it under the pink pillow of Sally's bed. "I'm sure you won't need it, though," she added. "My Sally is in the best of hands."

"Of course she is." Jessica beamed, feeling totally relaxed now that her sister was holding the dog bed and looking so capable. She was always certain things would go smoothly when Elizabeth was involved. "We really have to go now. I promised my family I'd bring Sally right home. Everyone is dying to see her."

"Very well, dear. I'll call later to say good night to Sally. She likes to hear my voice just before she goes to sleep." Mrs. Bramble handed her Sally's leash, and Jessica suddenly found herself being pulled sharply toward the door. The dog wanted to go out and was obviously used to getting her way.

All Jessica's composure vanished in an instant. The leash felt as if it were being tugged by a cyclone. Just when everything was going so well! The last thing she needed was to lose control of Sally and end up chasing her all over the house. She had to do something fast.

"Oh, Lizzie! Look at you, all loaded down." Jessica quickly handed the leash back to Mrs. Bramble and ran to her twin's side, grabbing the huge straw basket from her. "Why don't *you* take the doggie, while *I* help you with this heavy old thing." She yanked the dog bed out of Elizabeth's arms with such force that a box of Puppy Pops and a rubber lamb chop fell to the floor.

That was all Sally needed. Jerking the leash from Mrs. Bramble's hand and squeezing between Jessica's legs to reach the fallen chop, Sally moved faster than Jessica would have imagined possible. When she felt the animal dart between her feet, it was too much even for an accomplished actress like Jessica.

Screaming as if she'd been attacked by vampires, Jessica dropped the dog bed and covered her face with her hands. "Liz!" she shrieked. "Help! Help!"

Fortunately the big bed narrowly missed Sally's tail. The dog proceeded to pick up her toy and return to Jessica, wagging her tail. She dropped the squeaky chop at her new sitter's feet and waited expectantly for Jessica to continue the game.

But Jessica was in no mood for games. She stood still, her eyes covered and her body shaking with genuine fear. Elizabeth stopped quickly to pick up the fallen bed. She knew she couldn't let Mrs. Bramble discover the real cause of Jessica's distress.

"Did you drop this heavy bed on your toe, Jess?" she asked her twin. "I'll bet that hurt. Why don't you try walking around outside until it stops throbbing?"

Gratefully, Jessica rushed out of the house, while Mrs. Bramble bustled into the kitchen to get an ice pack. Elizabeth played inside with Sally. Minutes later, limping bravely, Jessica insisted that she didn't need the ice. Finally, with more last-minute instructions from Mrs. Bramble and Elizabeth holding Sally's leash, they started for home.

"Elizabeth Wakefield, you are a lifesaver!" Jessica was smiling again as they left Shady Dale Court and turned toward their own street. "What would I ever do without you?" It wasn't the first time she had asked that question, and somehow, Elizabeth was sure it wouldn't be the last.

Sally made herself at home with the Wakefields immediately. Mrs. Wakefield put the dog bed in a corner of the kitchen, and Mr. Wakefield found an old shag throw rug to cover the slippery floor. Steven collected sticks from the yard so he could play fetch with Sally, and Elizabeth poured fresh water in Sally's red bowl beside the bed.

The only Wakefield who didn't fuss over the new arrival was the one being paid to care for her. Jessica kept remembering how Sally had broken free and frightened her at Mrs. Bramble's. Now that there was no need to pretend that she dearly loved animals, she began to treat the dog as if it had a disease.

When it was time to feed Sally, Jessica discovered that the smell of dog food turned her stomach. She begged and pleaded until Elizabeth agreed to feed her instead. When it was time to take Sally for her evening walk, Jessica suddenly remembered all the homework she'd been putting off. "Goodness, Liz," she told her twin, "you're so good with Sally and such a whiz at science, I bet you could take care of both before poor old me has even finished answering my first question."

The next morning was no different from the night before. Jessica was the last one down for breakfast, and Sally, anxious for her first walk, met the sleepy girl with her leash in her mouth. At that very moment, though, Jessica remembered she was supposed to be at school early. She slipped a piece of toast from her plate, gathered up her books, gave her mother and father hurried kisses on the cheek and flew out the door.

"Cross my heart," she announced hurriedly, "I'll walk our cute little guest the minute I get home from school. But right now I have an urgent meeting." Jessica left a confused Sally whimpering at the door. "Pretty please, Steven. Walk her for me this morning? I'll love you forever."

"I'll bet," grumbled her brother, picking up Sally's leash. As he and the dog left for their walk, they watched Jessica disappear across the backyard. It was the first time Steven had ever seen his sister anxious to get to school.

Jessica's "meeting" was with the Unicorns. Although the seventh- and eighth-graders usually controlled the club, today it was Jessica who was the center of attention.

"Hi, Jessica," called Janet Howell as soon as she caught sight of Jessica. "Lila says you two bought your tickets to the concert yesterday. How would you both like a ride with me?"

"I thought there wasn't enough room," Jessica reminded her. She couldn't figure out why the snobbish club president was suddenly so considerate.

"Well, one rider can't go, and I just thought it would be great to meet Johnny with you after the show. After all, I *am* the Unicorn president, so I should probably welcome him to Sweet Valley."

"Hey, Jessica." The voice came from behind them, and all the girls turned to see Bruce Patman walking up the steps. He was wearing a football jersey that was much too big for him, but Jessica thought he looked cute anyway.

"I hear you've got a connection with The Buck." Bruce was looking straight at Jessica now. It was as if none of the other Unicorns even existed. "Caroline Pearce told Alex Betner you can get his whole band's autographs. How about you and me having a Coke at intermission?"

Thanks to gossipy Caroline, everyone in school knew about Jessica's letter to her idol. She smiled at Bruce. "I'd like that," she told him.

"News sure travels fast." Janet sneered. "How would Caroline Pearce know anything anyway? She's not even a Unicorn."

"Maybe not," commented Lila. "But that doesn't stop her from knowing everything about everybody. I'll bet she already knows what we all had for breakfast this morning."

"Big deal," Bruce added as the first bell rang. "I can tell you all something about lunch, and school hasn't even started yet."

"Really?" Jessica asked, impressed.

"Yup. It's going to make everyone sick." The second bell sounded, and the Unicorns pushed through the big oak doors, laughing and crowding around Jessica and Bruce. As Bruce walked with her down the hall, Jessica felt so happy she could burst.

Her excitement over the concert lasted all day long, until the twins came home exhausted from their Thursday-afternoon ballet class. No sooner had Jessica plopped down her books and reached for a bunch of grapes on the kitchen table than Sally jumped up on her lap with a bark that needed no translation.

"Oh, no!" wailed Jessica. "She wants to go for a walk. What'll I do?"

"Take her." Elizabeth laughed. "If you don't, we're liable to have a very wet floor and a very angry mother!"

"But, Liz, I just can't. I have this horrible pain in my side after all that dancing. I don't think I can walk a step." Jessica studied her sister, then winced as if her pain were too much to bear. "Do you think you could take her for me, Lizzie?" She knew from experience that if she begged with just the right amount of urgency, Elizabeth almost never said no. "Just this once?"

Elizabeth, on the other hand, knew from experience that Jessica's "pains" usually appeared whenever there was work to do. But the dog looked so shaggy and dear, she decided that a walk in the Sweet Valley twilight might be more fun than arguing with her twin.

As Elizabeth and Sally started off, the phone rang. Despite the twinge in her side just a moment before, Jessica dashed to the phone with the speed of an Olympic gymnast. "Hello," she said eagerly, hoping it was Lila to discuss Saturday's plans.

"Hello, dear," Mrs. Bramble's sweet old voice answered. "I'm just calling to see how you and Sally are getting along."

"Oh," Jessica sighed, trying not to sound too disappointed. "Your doggie's just fine. She loves her walks, and she's eating really well. I just can't tell you how crazy I am about her."

"Wonderful. I knew I wouldn't have anything to worry about. I'll just tell her good night and then let you go."

"Sally can't come to the phone now, Mrs. Bramble. She's out walking with my sister," said Jessica. "I had to sit this one out. I'm afraid I can't walk too well."

"I'm so sorry, dear. Is that toe still bothering you? Well, don't you worry. Sally and I are going to make it up to you. I've bought you a little surprise I'm bringing back with me."

"Oh, Mrs. Bramble," bubbled Jessica. "You shouldn't have. Besides, all Sally and I want is to see you back bright and early Saturday."

"I can't wait to see you both. Good night, dear."

Jessica's side felt fine until dinner was over and it was time for homework. Then, as her math assignment got more difficult, her muscles ached more and more. She had chewed her way through a whole bag of corn chips and broken two pencil points before she decided to get some help.

Opening the door to her twin's room, she saw Elizabeth hard at work, the bright desk light shining across her English book. "Gosh, Liz," she said, peering over her sister's shoulder, "you've finished your math already. You're so much better at word problems than I am. I think that if I worked the rest of my life I'd never be as good as you."

Elizabeth heard a familiar tone in her sister's voice. "If you're working your way up to asking me to help you with your math homework, Jess, the answer is no. How will you ever get better if you always get me to do all your problems for you?"

Jessica put her arms around her twin. "Oh, Lizzie, I wouldn't ask you unless I absolutely, positively had to. But unless you help me with my math, I'll never get my science or English done. And if I don't get my other subjects finished, I'll have to stay after school tomorrow. And if I stay after school, I'll get home too late to walk poor old Sally. And if I get home too late to walk Sally, you'll end up doing it for me."

She pulled Elizabeth from her chair and skipped toward her room. "I just couldn't let you do that again. After all, Sally is my responsibility. You wouldn't want me to let Mrs. Bramble down, would you?"

Elizabeth smiled as she followed her twin into

the pink-and-white bedroom. She had to admit that no one in the world was better at thinking up reasons for other people to do her work!

"If you'll do this for me, big sister, I'll be eternally grateful. What . . ."

"I know, I know," interrupted Elizabeth, wiping the corn chips off Jessica's math book. "What would you do without me?"

Six

◇

Saturday morning, Jessica woke with a delicious feeling of excitement. But instead of getting out of bed, she snuggled deeper into her pink sheets and daydreamed about the concert that afternoon. She imagined standing near the stage as Johnny Buck finished his last song. She saw the famous singer walk toward her to sign the cap and pictured the look of amazement on Janet Howell's face. Maybe, if Janet let her lead Booster cheers for a week, Jessica thought gleefully, she would allow the Unicorn president to hold the cap with Johnny's precious signature!

How would he autograph it, Jessica wondered, turning lazily onto her side to stare at the hat beside her stereo. Maybe he would write, "Yours always," or better yet, "With all my love." No matter what he chose, Jessica knew she would treasure his signature forever, absolutely forever. She'd never wash the cap, no matter how old it got. No matter how frayed and worn, it would always be her most prized possession.

Her daydreams were interrupted by a scratching sound just outside the bedroom door. Reluctantly, she sat up, pushed a tousled lock of blond hair from her eyes, and announced in a sleepy voice, "Come on in."

"Oh, no!" she shrieked as Sally pushed her fat body through the door and dropped her leash on Jessica's ruffled spread. "I take it back. Go away!" She burrowed again under the sheets, but soon felt sharp claws digging into her shoulders.

Racing downstairs with Sally in pursuit, Jessica was dismayed to find not a single Wakefield in sight. Obviously, she had slept late and missed her father's departure for his out-of-town case. And her mother had already gone to meet her important clients.

"Steven? Elizabeth? Where *is* everybody?" She flopped disconsolately into a chair at the table, where a half-eaten breakfast and an empty plate were the only evidence that she even had a brother and sister.

Jessica stared at Sally, and Sally stared at Jessica. Jessica decided she felt a serious stomach ache coming on. She was definitely in no condition for dog-walking. But Sally took matters into her own paws. The leash in her mouth, she ran to the back door and began scratching at it furiously.

Suddenly, the door flew open, sending a startled Sally scurrying backward to the kitchen table. In ran three laughing girls, and one of them, much to Jessica's relief, was Elizabeth.

"Oh, Liz. Thank goodness you're back. I have a terrible stomach ache and Monster here was about to rip the door off its hinges."

"Sorry, Jess. Amy, Julie, and I have a date at Casey's." Jessica's twin ran to the closet, grabbed her purse, and headed back to the door. "We've been working on the paper all morning, and I promised everyone ice-cream sundaes. We're already late. Caroline Pearce, our gossip columnist, is meeting us there."

Julie Porter, a small graceful girl with wavy red hair, stopped to pet Sally. "What a darling dog." In no time at all, her pretty face was covered with dog kisses. "And so friendly, too!"

"*Too* friendly, if you ask me." Jessica pouted. She clutched her stomach and looked around the room for sympathy. "You know," she suggested miserably, "I really think I'm allergic to dog hair."

"That's the only thing that could explain why you get sick whenever it's time for Sally's walk." Elizabeth laughed.

"Say, maybe you should take her with you." Jessica brightened at the thought. "I bet a friendly dog like Sally would just love a walk downtown."

"No luck," answered her sister, letting Amy out the door in front of her. "You know they don't allow dogs in Casey's."

"Not according to Bruce Patman," insisted Julie, following close behind. "He says they've got lots of them working behind the counter!"

The three friends broke out into giggles, then started out the door, leaving Jessica alone again with Sally. It looked as if the two of them were finally going on their first walk together. Fearfully recalling Sally's escape at Mrs. Bramble's, Jessica wrapped the end of the dog's leash around her hand three times and headed bravely out the front door.

It was a beautiful day. The sky had just traces of fluffy clouds and the street was full of people enjoying the sunny California weather. At every turn, Jessica met another neighbor who stopped to exclaim over the friendly dust mop that was tugging her briskly down the sidewalk.

"What a darling dog!" said one.

"What a cute little doggie!" exclaimed another.

"How dear!" declared Mrs. Pearce, the Wakefields' two-doors-down neighbor.

Jessica had become so used to hearing Sally praised by every passerby that she was surprised when a tall girl her own age walked past them without a word. In fact, she hadn't even glanced at Sally, who had wriggled and wagged her tail, expecting the usual friendly comments.

At first, Jessica was pleased. *That's the only sensible person we've met*, she thought to herself, glancing back at the perfectly groomed girl. Not a hair seemed out of place, and even though it was the weekend, the girl was wearing a straight skirt, stockings, and a pretty quilted jacket.

Sally, however, felt quite differently about being ignored. Tugging at the leash, she strained backward, begging to go to the girl. In fact, when she suddenly began barking loudly, it looked as if she might get her way. The girl turned and looked toward Jessica and the yapping spaniel.

"Hello." Jessica smiled in friendly greeting. "I'm Jessica Wakefield."

"I'm Brooke Dennis, and that dog of yours really needs a bath."

Jessica, who was not a member of Sally's fan club, was still upset by the girl's bluntness. "How would you know?" she asked. "You barely looked at *her*."

"My mother used to raise show dogs, so I know what to look for. And, believe me, that dog's not *worth* looking at."

Brooke started to walk on, but Sally did not consider the interview over. She had worked her way to the stranger and now began trying to change her mind by licking her ankles.

"Ugh! Get this mangy mutt off of me!" Brooke jumped back, pushing Sally away with her foot.

"Don't you kick my dog!" Jessica was angry in spite of herself. "Sally may need a bath, but you could use some manners."

"Oh, brother." The girl rolled her eyes as if Jessica were the stupidest person alive. "I sure am sorry I'm moving to this dumb town." She turned and strode off down the street.

To her horror, Jessica watched the girl turn up the walkway to the Logginses' old house. It was one of the loveliest homes in the neighborhood and had been for sale since the Logginses had moved to New York. Now, a huge moving-van was parked in the driveway, and it seemed the Wakefields were about to get a very unpleasant neighbor!

Sally and Jessica continued their walk, meeting nothing but kindness from the rest of the people they passed. By the time Jessica decided it was time to start home, she had all but forgotten about Brooke Dennis. Once again she was tired of listening to everyone make such a fuss over Mrs. Bramble's pet. Still she was relieved that Sally was obedient, and not once had Jessica felt in any danger of losing her charge.

That is, until they met Mrs. Blaney's cat just three blocks from home. The cat was huge and black and not at all fond of dogs, particularly friendly ones like Sally. Before Jessica knew what had happened, the cat had scratched Sally's nose. Sally had turned from an ancient cocker spaniel into a streak of brown lightning. With Jessica holding desperately to her leash, the old dog tore across the Blaney yard hard on the trail of her tormentor.

All thoughts of Johnny Buck and the concert that afternoon vanished. Now Jessica had only one goal—to hold on to the leash that was jerking her over hedges and across streets in a frantic zigzag. The cat was very large, but it was an agile runner. It was at least five minutes before Jessica and Sally stood panting under a stately oak tree. Up above them, in the highest branches, sat the cat, looking as if it had chosen the spot for its Saturday nap.

"My poor little Tabbatha! Someone help my Tabby!"

Mrs. Blaney ran toward them, her arms flapping wildly. She had obviously watched the wild chase from her yard and had no idea how capable her "little Tabbatha" was of taking care of herself.

"Oh, goodness!" She stood wringing her hands under the big tree. "Look what that nasty dog of yours has done. How is Tabby ever going to get down from there?"

"I'm awfully sorry." Jessica caught her breath and started to explain. "You see, your cat scratched Sally, and Sally started chasing her, and . . ."

"Nonsense!" Mrs. Blaney interrupted. "Tabbatha's never scratched anyone in her life!" She looked as though Jessica has accused one of her children of doing something dreadfully wrong. "Why, I don't even need to put a bell on my baby. She's such a good cat, she doesn't bother the birds at all."

Jessica had her own suspicions about what Tabbatha did when Mrs. Blaney wasn't looking. But she decided it was best to let Mrs. Blaney put the blame on Sally if they ever hoped to get home in peace. It was nearly twelve o'clock, and Mrs. Bramble would be returning any minute. After all, it wouldn't matter who had scratched whom once Jessica was sitting by Secca Lake, listening to Johnny Buck belt out his big hits.

"Maybe," she suggested to her worried neighbor, "your kitty likes it up in that tree." She studied Tabbatha, who was sprawled like a black tiger across a leafy branch. "I bet she'll come down when she's finished napping."

Mrs. Blaney placed a stray wisp of gray hair back into her bun. She squinted through the sunlight into the tree. "I don't think so," she said uncertainly. "She's never been up so high. I'm afraid we'll have to call the police."

The police! Jessica could just imagine the uproar once a police car arrived on the scene! Mrs.

Bramble would never forgive her and, worse still, Jessica would never get to Lila's house on time. She had to get Sally home as quickly as possible. The only way to do that was to coax Tabbatha down from the tree.

"Oh, there's no need to scare Tabby with the police," Jessica told Mrs. Blaney. "I'm sure she's almost ready to come down. Here, Kitty. Here, Kitty," Jessica called up into the tree. She watched the cat turn over lazily and shut its eyes. How was she ever going to trick it down?

Mrs. Blaney, determined to aid her helpless pet, started for her house to phone the authorities. Suddenly, Jessica had a brainstorm. "Wait," she called out, fumbling through her pockets for the rubber lamb chop she had put there when they came outside. "I can get her down for you," she told Mrs. Blaney.

"Tabbatha!" Jessica yelled up to the tree. "Come down, and Sally will give you her funny toy." She squeezed the rubber chop over and over again until it sounded as though a flock of baby chicks had settled at the base of the tree.

Tabbatha peered down at Jessica and Sally, her green eyes suddenly wide open. Jessica, growing more hopeful with every squeak, handed the dog leash to Mrs. Blaney. "Here," she urged. "You take Sally out of sight around the corner, and we'll have your Tabby down in just no time."

For a gentle cat who never chased birds, Tabbatha was incredibly fascinated by the tiny, squeaking toy. As soon as Sally and Mrs. Blaney had disappeared from view, she began inching her way slowly down the tree trunk. "Here, Kitty,"

Jessica called softly as she squeezed the chop. "Here, Kitty, Kitty."

At the bottom of the tree, Tabbatha was rewarded with the dog toy, which she promptly snatched up in her mouth and carried off to the Blaneys' backyard. Jessica was certain she could explain the missing toy somehow, so she grabbed Sally's leash from Mrs. Blaney and rushed home.

As she and Sally walked into the kitchen, the Wakefields' phone started to ring. *It must be Mrs. Bramble,* thought Jessica. She answered in a voice she hoped sounded like that of a mature and efficient dog-sitter.

"Why do you sound so funny?" asked Lila Fowler. "And why aren't you over here yet? I can't wait to show you the new outfit Daddy let me pick out for the concert!"

Lila's excitement was contagious. After her busy morning, Jessica was more than ready to think about important things like what she would wear to see Johnny Buck. "I'm coming just as soon as Sally's owner gets back," she told Lila. "In the meantime, tell me all about it. I'm dying to hear."

"It's really outrageous, Jess. Daddy took one look and said I'd wear it over his dead body. It's perfect!"

Jessica, who knew it would take at least three of her own closets to accommodate Lila's huge wardrobe, was impressed. "It sounds terrific, Lila. But how did you get your father to let you wear it?"

"I just told him that if the *clothes* I picked out upset him—" Lila giggled. "Wait till he gets the *bill!*"

Jessica admired the way Lila had always been

able to wrap her father around her little finger. Of course, she realized, Lila spent a lot less time with her father than Jessica and Elizabeth did with theirs. And Jessica always ended by deciding she wouldn't want to trade dads with *anyone*!

The minute she and Lila had hung up, Jessica dialed the little house on Shady Dale Court. Perhaps, she told herself anxiously, Mrs. Bramble had called while she and Sally were out walking. The phone company commercials always said to let a phone ring ten times, so Jessica let it ring twenty times before she decided that Mrs. Bramble still wasn't back from her trip.

There was no time to lose. Jessica decided to pick out her clothes for the concert and pack so that she'd be ready the minute Mrs. Bramble called. In all the excitement that day, she'd barely given a thought to the outfit she was going to wear. Now Jessica began to realize the horrible truth. In her whole set of drawers, in her entire closet, there wasn't a shred of clothing that was right for this very special occasion!

Frantically, she opened every drawer in her dresser and threw sweaters and blouses onto the floor in a colorful heap. Groaning with each new item she pulled out, Jessica had soon cleaned out every drawer. One tearful look at her closet convinced her that nothing there was worthy of Johnny Buck. At last Jessica remembered that there was a whole roomful of outfits she hadn't even considered.

Jessica rushed into Elizabeth's bedroom, opened her twin's closet, and scanned the rack with an eagle eye. She immediately eliminated all the old, familiar clothes she'd borrowed so many times before. Then she saw what she was looking for. Pushed to one side, still in its transparent wrapper from Kendall's, was the new dress Elizabeth had bought for the sixth-grade dance.

It was a pale beige with a scoop neck and a raspberry jacket. Underneath it, on the floor, was a pair of soft leather slippers that were absolutely perfect. Quickly, Jessica slipped into the shoes and carried the dress to the mirror. Since she and Elizabeth wore the same size there was no need to try it on. When she held it up and saw how perfectly the jacket highlighted her golden hair, and how well the shoes matched the dress, she knew what she'd wear that afternoon. And, even though she didn't have time to ask her twin about borrowing the outfit, she was certain that Elizabeth would want her to look her best for the biggest moment of her life. After all, who would even think of comparing a middle-school dance to a date with Johnny Buck?

As she twirled confidently in front of the mirror, Jessica realized there was still something missing. She needed a necklace or bracelet to add the finishing touch. She crossed the room to Elizabeth's jewelry box and began to rummage through the silver bracelets and brightly colored earrings.

That was when Jessica spotted the small gray box. Gently opening the hinged top, she found the huge gold hoops that Elizabeth had bought their mother for her birthday. Cushioned in the gray velvet, they sparkled. And, the more she stared at those dazzling earrings, the more convinced Jessica became that they were made for her new outfit.

If the concert hadn't been so important, Jessica would never have considered borrowing the earrings. But she was convinced that her mother, like Elizabeth, wanted the very best for her. And the best meant looking right for Johnny and turning Lila Fowler green with envy. Besides, she told herself, slipping the hoops onto her ears, she would have them safely back in the little gray box before anyone even missed them.

As she was packing her overnight bag, the phone rang. Jessica felt wonderfully relieved to hear Mrs. Bramble's voice when she answered.

But Mrs. Bramble had bad news. Her bus had had some mechanical difficulties. She and the other passengers had been shuttled back to the bus depot to wait for the next bus south. And they were still waiting.

"I'm sorry, dear. But they can't schedule another bus for Sweet Valley until two-thirty. It looks as if I'll have to wait until later tonight to see you and Sally."

"But that's too late!" Jessica's voice sounded angry in spite of herself, and her turquoise eyes welled with tears.

"Too late?"

"I—I mean, Sally misses you terribly, and—and I promised her you'd be home for lunch."

"Well, I am as sorry as she is, dear. But we'll just have to make up for it with a special treat tonight. See you then." Mrs. Bramble hung up, and Jessica ran into her own room. She slammed the door, collapsed onto her bed, and cried as if her heart would break.

Seven

◇

But Jessica Wakefield wasn't the kind to give up easily. She had worked too hard for this day to let a change in plans destroy everything. Soon she stopped crying and started plotting. Nothing was going to stop her from seeing Johnny Buck.

After all, she reasoned, she had already finished the job Mrs. Bramble had paid her for. And ever since her confrontation with Tabbatha, Jessica felt she had earned every penny! Steven was going to the concert, too, but Elizabeth would be home soon. Her twin could watch Sally for a few hours, and then explain to Mrs. Bramble that Jessica had made plans to spend the night with Lila. She was sure her sister could make Sally's owner understand.

Jessica carefully folded Elizabeth's new dress and tucked it into her overnighter. With the final additions of a toothbrush and the small gray jewel box, her bag was packed. Jessica Wakefield was ready for the most thrilling moment any girl could ever hope for. She could already see Johnny's handsome face and hear his tremendous voice as she dashed downstairs to wait for Elizabeth to come home.

She watched the clock impatiently until it was nearly two-thirty—just an hour and a half before the concert was scheduled to begin. Still there was no sign of Elizabeth. Jessica's only company was Sally, who stood panting hoarsely by her water dish. Her mad cat-chase must have made the old dog thirsty, Jessica finally realized. Sally's sides were heaving, and she sounded like a tired vacuum cleaner.

"All right, all right," she told Sally. "I'll give you some water, but then I'm leaving, and you'll just have to take care of yourself until Aunt Elizabeth gets here!"

As she talked, Jessica filled the red bowl with water from the sink. Then, setting it by the huffing spaniel, she watched Sally finish the entire bowl in less than a minute. Jessica had never seen water disappear so fast before.

"You were thirstier than I thought," she said, filling the bowl again. Once again, Sally drank it all and once more, Jessica filled it to the top. "Three bowls of water," she told Sally when the dog finally raised her head, looking for more, "are enough for a dog twice your size. It's a wonder you don't burst!"

Suddenly Jessica stopped and clapped her hand over her mouth. "Oh, my gosh! Burst is right! What am I going to do? I can't let you wait for Elizabeth inside. If I leave you here, you'll ruin the carpets." She looked anxiously at Sally, whose little stomach had already begun to look like an inflated balloon.

If Jessica stayed at home any longer, she'd never have time to dress at Lila's. Besides, she knew how important it was to get to the concert early. Half the fun would be meeting her friends and finding out where they were sitting. She wanted everyone from school to see her get Johnny's autograph. She watched Sally waddle toward the door and knew she couldn't let that hairy water balloon spoil everything!

"OK," Jessica decided aloud. "You want to go out? Out we go!" She found a length of clothesline in the broom closet and, fastening one end of the rope to Sally's collar, led the dog into the backyard. Holding the other end of the clothesline like a leash, Jessica surveyed the yard for the biggest tree she could find.

The old pine would do perfectly. When they were younger, both twins loved the huge tree and spent countless hours in the cool shadows of its lowest branches. Elizabeth still liked to take her favorite books to one thick branch she called her "thinking seat." Jessica thought it was a perfect place for Sally.

As Sally stood patiently, Jessica tried to remember what Steven had shown her about knots after his Boy Scout jamboree. But all she recalled was the way he had howled with laughter whenever she tried any of the knots he showed her. Oh, well, it would just have to be a plain old knot. Besides, Sally was so tired from her morning romp, she'd probably be content just to lie quietly under the pine until Elizabeth came home.

Jessica wrapped the long cord once around the tree, tied it as best she could, and darted back into the kitchen to write a hurried note to her sister. Then, without so much as a goodbye for Sally, she was off.

The dog, however, barely noticed Jessica's absence. Very soon she had plenty to occupy her attention, especially when she spotted a dark shadow moving along the white wall by the flower garden. If it weren't for the screeching birds and a very familiar scent, the old cocker spaniel would probably not have recognized Tabbatha. As soon as she did, though, Jessica's hastily tied knot was no match for the fur fireball that broke free and shot after the prowling cat.

When Elizabeth walked into the empty kitchen after her lunch at Casey's, she was surprised not to hear Sally barking her usual greeting. Then she remembered that this was the day Mrs. Bramble was coming home. She assumed that Sally had already gone back to Shady Dale Court. It wasn't until she noticed the wicker dog bed still nestled in the corner and Sally's leash still hanging from the coatrack that Elizabeth began to worry.

She grew even more concerned when she found Jessica's note, fastened to the refrigerator with a magnet. "Liz," Jessica had written, "Mrs. Bramble won't be back to pick up Fuzz-Ball until after dinner. Please be a pal and watch Sally for a few hours. I know you can fix things with Mrs. B." There was a long row of x's across the bottom of the paper, and Jessica had signed her name with a tiny heart instead of a dot above the "i."

Now Elizabeth began to look everywhere for the dog. "Sally!" she called, opening every door in the house, in case the spaniel had gotten locked in someone's room by mistake. One by one, she checked the upstairs bedrooms and bathrooms. Downstairs, she peered into every corner of the living room, dining room, and den. She opened the door to her father's study, and even looked inside the bottom drawer of Mr. Wakefield's big metal file cabinet. But Sally wasn't there or anywhere else.

Finally Elizabeth went outside and began to circle the house slowly. "Sally!" she called into the flower bed. "Sally!" she yelled as she checked the swimming-pool gate. When she found the rope around the pine tree, she knew she had to try to reach Jessica.

Someone at Lila's house certainly liked to talk on the telephone! Elizabeth called the Fowlers' number six times and got a busy signal each time. At last, she decided she'd rather walk to the house than waste any more time trying to phone.

A few minutes later, Elizabeth reached Lila's house. She took a deep breath, knocked loudly on the great oak door and waited for the housekeeper to answer.

A tall woman opened the door and told Elizabeth that Lila and Jessica had left moments before when their ride came. Elizabeth was even more disappointed when she learned that they would not be back until eight-thirty.

Elizabeth thanked the housekeeper and watched quietly as the polished marble floor and circular staircase disappeared behind the heavy door.

Standing alone outside the beautiful home, Elizabeth was glad no one could see the tears of frustration in her eyes. How could Jessica do such a thing? How could she be so careless? Mrs. Bramble would be back for Sally before Jessica returned to Lila's house, and it would be Elizabeth who would have to face her. What could she possibly say?

Elizabeth knew she needed help if she was ever going to find Sally. As soon as she reached home, she called Amy Sutton and told her the bad news. She asked her friend to ride over on her bike as quickly as possible. It was nearly four-thirty now, and they had only a few hours at most to find Sally.

When Amy arrived on her ten-speed, Elizabeth could have kissed her. She knew she could count on her friend's help, no matter what the problem. And, at a time like this, it made Elizabeth feel better just to know Amy was there.

The girls decided to comb the neighborhood by bike, ringing doorbells and searching the yards of every house they passed. The two friends agreed that Sally was too old to have wandered very far.

After an hour and a half, they were thoroughly exhausted. They had ridden until their legs ached, and everyone within a ten-block radius of the Wakefield house knew that sad story.

But no one had seen the dog. Mrs. Blaney, of course, remembered Sally from that morning, but she hadn't seen a trace of the dog all afternoon.

"I guess it's no use," Elizabeth admitted at last. "Sally's really lost."

"I'm awfully sorry, Liz," said Amy. "So is everyone else in the neighborhood. I even had three people offer to look for her."

"Yes," agreed Elizabeth. "Everyone's been really kind—all except for a girl at the Logginses' house."

"What do you mean?"

"I rang the doorbell to ask about Sally. The girl who answered said she'd already told me my dog should stay lost, and she hoped it did!"

"Boy! That's weird. But one thing's for sure, Elizabeth. It's getting dark, and Sally is nowhere in sight."

"Well, I'll just have to go home and face facts." Elizabeth turned her bike toward the house. "And so will Jessica, as soon as Mom gets back!" She hated to think of what would happen when her mother returned from her meeting and discovered Sally was gone. Elizabeth was certain she'd insist on calling Lila's house to get Jessica. Once that happened, her twin's secret trip to Johnny Buck's concert was sure to be found out.

As angry as Elizabeth was with Jessica for her latest caper, she knew her twin would never deliberately plan to hurt anyone—even Sally. It was just that once Jessica had her heart set on something, she usually forgot about everything else. But, for all her faults, her twin had always been someone Elizabeth was proud of.

After riding back to Amy's house, Elizabeth quickly headed home. As she rounded the last corner and the Wakefield house came into view, her worst fears were realized. There, sitting in the driveway, clearly visible in the soft twilight, was her mother's car! Tired and discouraged, Elizabeth put her bike in the garage and trudged into the kitchen. It was time to explain the latest mess that Jessica had left her to clean up.

Eight

◇

"I hope you brought your binoculars," Lila shouted over the din of the crowd at Secca Lake. "Because you'll need them to tell the difference between Johnny and the rest of the band."

Lila was right. From where the girls sat, the stagehands who were setting up looked like tiny black ants!

"It's OK," Jessica insisted. "We'll still be able to hear that dreamy voice!" But as Johnny and his band ran onto the stage, the sea of fans around the girls exploded into such thunderous applause that it was impossible to hear anything. Jessica strained forward to catch a glimpse of Johnny, but found that until he walked to the microphone, she couldn't distinguish him from any of the other five tiny figures who stood at the microphones.

Suddenly yellow and green lasers of light shot across the stage, and The Buck, dressed in black, began his first song. It was "Saturday Blues," a fast, funny romp that Jessica, Lila, and all the Unicorns loved.

For a few minutes Jessica closed her eyes, listening to Johnny's soft, sweet voice and feeling as if The Buck were beside her.

She squeezed her friend's hand. "Isn't he just too much?" she squealed. "Isn't he just too fabulous for words?"

Lila, too, was thrilled. She smiled at Jessica and then turned back toward the stage, a sleepy, dreamy expression on her face. Before the first song ended, though, both girls had stopped smiling. Johnny's microphone had gone dead!

Three men rushed onto the stage and began to tug frantically at the tiny microphone. Then two more men raced to the forest of standing mikes by the drummer and started untangling the black wires that snaked across the floor. At last, a sixth man walked to the center of the stage and held up his hands. His mouth opened and closed silently, and he seemed to be begging the crowd to be patient.

But they weren't. Jessica looked around her. People were hunched forward as if they could hear better by leaning toward the distant stage. Some fans were yelling and stamping their feet, while others were demanding their money back. One woman, seated right behind Lila and Jessica, shouted a string of swearwords that stunned everyone around her into silence for several seconds.

Soon, though, the impatient crowd became noisy again, and Jessica grabbed Lila's hand. "We've got to get closer," she told her friend. "If we start moving now, we can be right next to the stage for intermission. Don't forget, we've got some serious autograph hunting to do." With her precious hat in one hand, she began pulling Lila from her seat with the other.

But Lila was unnerved by the angry throng of people all around them. "If you want to fight that mob, Jessica Wakefield, you're going to have to do it alone. I'm staying right where I am."

Jessica knew from experience that there was no point in trying to persuade Lila to do anything she didn't want to do. But she was just as sure that a few thousand people weren't going to stand between her and Johnny Buck. Spotting a boy in the crowd who looked just like Bruce Patman, Jessica stepped out into the aisle.

After working her way slowly forward through the crowd, Jessica realized that the boy she had thought was Bruce was in fact a boy she didn't know at all. He was staring so intently at the stage that he didn't even notice Jessica or even the girl who had her arm around his shoulder.

Discouraged, Jessica turned to rejoin Lila. But she had lost sight of her friend in the crowd. Johnny's microphone had been fixed, and people everywhere were standing at their seats now, swaying and moving to the music as he sang. In the waves of people around her, there was no way Jessica could pick out Lila.

Intermission made matters worse. The crowd began to move around, to stretch their legs, and head for rest areas and refreshment stands. Jessica gave up trying to find Lila and instead let herself be carried toward the now-empty stage. She was certain that if she just kept moving forward, she would eventually reach Johnny. It was slow going and, in the thick of the crowd, Jessica could see little more than the heads of the people in front of her. When she suddenly felt a hand on her shoulder, she whirled around, frightened. It was Bruce Patman, smiling broadly, as cool and confident as ever.

"Hi, Jess."

Jessica was relieved to see a familiar face. "Hi, Bruce. I've lost Lila in this awful crowd."

"Good. I thought you and I had a Coke date anyway."

Jessica brightened. She had noticed the two yellow refreshment tents set up on either side of the stage. If she and Bruce could work their way to one, she would be that much closer to Johnny.

"Fine! Let's go." She smiled and started following Bruce, who threaded his way smoothly through the crowd as if he knew exactly where he was going. Soon they were standing in a long line outside one of the huge tents. They inched their way forward until they were just outside the yellow flaps and Jessica could smell the hot pretzels and pizza.

That was when The Buck and his band leaped back onto the stage for the second half of their show. Purple and blue lights shot across the sky and over the crowd's heads, as the musicians swung into one of their most popular songs. Bruce grabbed Jessica's hand and stepped out of the food line. "He's singing 'Forever Fever'! That's my all-time favorite. Let's get back to our seats."

"No. I'm not going back." Jessica didn't care about locating Lila or eating pretzels or getting back to her seat. She had to reach Johnny before the end of the show. "I'm staying here. The Buck's going to sign my hat."

"Suit yourself. See you later." Bruce waved, turned back toward the grandstands, and was soon out of sight. Jessica faced the stage and began working her way through the crowd alone. She used the colorful beams of light like a compass to guide her toward the band, but without Bruce, she felt a lot less certain that she was headed in the right direction.

As she got nearer to the stage, Jessica noticed something strange. When she had left the round refreshment tent, she passed a small group of girls about her age. One of them was a pretty redhead who was watching The Buck with a look of rapture on her face. Clutched close to her chest with both hands, she held a hat exactly like the one Jessica was carrying!

Why had Johnny owned two identical hats? Jessica was perplexed, but she held her own souvenir still tighter and fought on through the sea of fans. Just then she spotted three more girls. They were yelling a cheer they had made up. "We love you, Johnny," they shouted together toward the stage. "We love your style. You've got them all beat by a mile!"

It wasn't their cheer that made Jessica stop and stare in disbelief at the trio of fans. It was the three striped caps the girls held in their hands and waved as they shouted. Each hat was exactly like the one Johnny had thrown to Jessica at the Valley View Hotel!

He must have given hats out like peanuts! Jessica fumed as she passed more and more fans with hats just like hers. She remembered how she had boasted about that silly hat, how she'd made a total fool of herself by insisting that Johnny Buck had meant his precious cap just for her! By the time The Buck was finishing his last number, she had managed to reach the front of the stage. She found herself surrounded by at least fifty screaming fans waving fifty striped caps.

That phony! Jessica exploded silently. He must have handed out dozens of caps in every town he visited. And now, Jessica was being jostled and shoved by a mob of girls, each thinking she had the most special souvenir in the world.

But as the music stopped and the lights faded, Jessica decided that if she could manage to get the cap signed by The Buck himself, it could still be a precious memento. If only Johnny would walk toward the stage apron, Jessica was sure she could make him realize how important it was that he sign her hat.

But she never even got a chance to ask Johnny for his autograph. The minute he bowed his head for applause, two huge bodyguards joined him onstage, one on each side of him, like burly bookends. After a final bow, The Buck walked off between them without even coming near the front of the stage. All around her, Jessica heard girls groaning and saw hundreds of caps, albums, and T-shirts waving frantically. "We want The Buck!" someone shouted from the crowd, and soon everyone had picked up the chant.

"We want The Buck! We want The Buck!" The foot-stamping, chanting and clapping were so insistent that Jessica began to hope Johnny might reappear after all. Suddenly the noise stopped as a figure strode onstage and approached the persistent group of fans. Unfortunately, it wasn't Johnny Buck. It was a small, fat man in a brown suit, who began handing out photographs of the young singer.

Sweating under the hot lights, the little man put picture after picture into the eager hands of the crowd that ringed the stage. Jessica found herself pushed forward so hard by the fans behind her that she had to brace herself against the back of a girl in front of her.

"Wait your turn!" The girl turned angrily to scold Jessica and, as she did, Jessica lost her footing and fell to the ground. Instead of jumping up again to fight for a picture, Jessica stayed where she had fallen. Sitting on the grass, now wet with dew, she put her head in her hands and cried in humiliation.

"Now, now. We can't have that. Here. Here's a special one just for you." The little man leaned into the crowd, and Jessica suddenly realized he was speaking to her. "Up you go, little miss. Help her up, folks." Jessica felt herself being lifted up by arms on all sides. She stood up, with a tear-stained face and a grass-stained dress, looking at the man.

"Here you go. Johnny signed this one just for you." He handed her one of the glossy photographs and then moved on down the rim of the stage to another group of fans.

"What's yours say?" The girl who had caused Jessica to fall seemed to have forgotten her annoyance and was peering curiously over her shoulder at Jessica's picture.

It was a black-and-white photograph that showed Johnny sitting in a hammock with his guitar. Scrawled across the corner in blue ink were the words, "Keep on rocking—from your friend, Johnny Buck." Yuck!

"Mine, too," said the girl, turning back to her own photo. Jessica knew without looking that everyone in the crowd around her now held a photograph of Johnny with the same inscription. Instead of a one-of-a-kind hat with "To Jessica, Love always, Johnny" written on the brim, she was stuck with a dumb picture and a stamped autograph. She had never felt so humiliated!

Or so lost. How was she going to find Lila? How was she ever going to live down this night? Why hadn't she listened to Elizabeth? Why wasn't she home right now, saying goodbye to Mrs. Bramble and hello to twenty-five dollars to spend on anything she wanted?

A gruff voice interrupted her thoughts.

"Where have you been? We've been looking everywhere for you." It was Janet's brother and he looked angry. "Didn't you remember we were all supposed to meet by the fountain after the show?" Jessica followed him gratefully.

Yes. Of course. Janet and the boys had arranged with Lila and Jessica to meet at the fountain if they lost one another. But Jessica had been so intent on her fantasy, she had forgotten all about it. Thank goodness Lila had not, and had sent the boys to find her. Jessica sank into the backseat of the Mustang and took a silent oath to

wait until she was twenty-one before going to another concert!

Everyone in the car was talking at once, and
all of them seemed to have had a terrific time.
Even Lila admitted that once the microphone was
fixed she had really loved the music and the light
show. "How about you?" she asked Jessica. "Did
you talk to Johnny?"

"Not exactly," muttered Jessica. "He didn't
have time."

"I figured as much." Janet sounded very su-
perior. Jessica felt ridiculous.

"But his assistant did tell me he signed this
picture especially for me." Hopefully, Jessica
handed the photo to Janet, who laughed loudly
and passed it on to the others.

"You bet he signed that just for you." Jessica
could see Janet's sneer even in the dark car. "For
you and about a thousand other people! I bought
the exact same picture in the refreshment tent."

Jessica studied the photograph Janet handed
her. There was Johnny in the hammock, and there
in the corner of the picture were the same dumb
words. Janet would never let her live *this* down.
Maybe, Jessica decided miserably, she should ask
her mother for a home tutor. Then she could
spend the rest of sixth grade in her room!

Her cheeks burning, Jessica sat quietly in the
dark car and, for the first time all night, thought of
Sally. How she wished she had stayed home, finished her job, and still had twenty-five dollars to
spend. If she had, she'd have a lot more money
and feel a lot less humiliation than she did right
now.

Nine

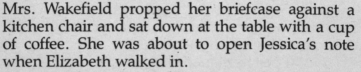

Mrs. Wakefield propped her briefcase against a kitchen chair and sat down at the table with a cup of coffee. She was about to open Jessica's note when Elizabeth walked in.

"Hi, there. Looks like it's just the two of us tonight. Want to celebrate my successful meeting with Chinese take-out?"

Elizabeth was glad her mother's day had gone well. But now it was that much harder to spoil everything with the bad news about Sally. "Maybe, Mom. But I have something to tell you first."

"Uh-oh. I know that look." Mrs. Wakefield carried her coffee cup to the sink to rinse it under the faucet. "Don't tell me Sally chewed up my curtains!"

"I wish that were all." Elizabeth sighed. "I'm afraid she's lost, Mom."

"*Who's* lost?"

"Sally."

Her mother listened quietly while Elizabeth

described the fruitless house-to-house search she and Amy had just conducted. She told her about the note and the rope and the whole horrible afternoon.

Of course, there was one detail Elizabeth didn't mention: The Buck's concert. So, although Jessica was in hot water for being careless, at least her parents didn't know she had also disobeyed them. Elizabeth couldn't bear to see her twin punished, even when she deserved it!

"I just don't understand why she couldn't have waited." The twins' mother seemed less angry than puzzled. "Jessica spends so much time with Lila, you'd think she could have waited a few hours."

"Maybe she promised the Fowlers she'd have dinner there," Elizabeth suggested.

"But she had already made a more important promise," Mrs. Wakefield insisted. "To Mrs. Bramble."

As if on cue, the door bell rang. Both Elizabeth and Mrs. Wakefield jumped. They looked at each other, knowing exactly who it must be. Neither of them wanted to answer the door. Finally Elizabeth greeted the elderly woman with an embarrassed smile.

"Hello, Mrs. Bramble. Please come in. My mother's in the kitchen."

"Hello, my dear. I really can't stay. I just wanted to thank you so much for watching my Sally. Oh, and here's the little gift I promised you." Mrs. Bramble took a tiny, gaily wrapped box from her suitcase and put it into Elizabeth's hands. Just then Elizabeth realized that Mrs. Bramble had mistaken her for her twin.

"I'm Elizabeth, Mrs. Bramble. But I'll give this to Jessica just as soon as she comes home. Won't you sit down?" Elizabeth steered their guest toward the living room. Somehow she thought it was important that Mrs. Bramble be sitting when she learned about Sally!

"No, thank you. I think I'll just pick up my old girl and take her right home. I think we must both be pretty tired."

Mrs. Wakefield joined them in the hall. "You *do* look exhausted," she told Mrs. Bramble. "It must have been an awful trip. I insist you come and sit down in the living room."

Mrs. Bramble settled at last into the sofa, telling them about the bus problem and the countless delays that followed. But she had finished only a few sentences before she stopped short.

"Enough about me." She laughed. "Let's hear about you and Sally. I just can't tell you how comforting it was to know she was staying with a lovely family like yours."

Again Elizabeth and her mother exchanged worried glances. Poor Mrs. Bramble was so sincere in her praise of the Wakefields that the two of them felt worse than ever. Elizabeth was grateful when her mother finally chose to be the one to break the news.

"I'm afraid one member of this family wasn't as responsible as she should have been, Mrs. Bramble. My daughter Jessica had made arrangements to visit a friend tonight, and when you were late, she decided not to change her plans."

"Oh, that's all right." Mrs. Bramble smiled kindly. "I know how young people are. I'm sure Sally will forgive her for not saying goodbye."

Mrs. Wakefield was obviously uncomfortable. Elizabeth watched her mother shift uneasily in her seat, then touch Mrs. Bramble's arm gently as she finished the sad story. "Jessica didn't wait for any of us to relieve her, Mrs. Bramble. She tied Sally to a tree in our backyard. She left her alone, and by the time Elizabeth came home, Sally had broken free and run off."

The little woman still didn't seem to understand what had happened. "Oh, she does like to run," she said. "Sometimes I have all I can do to keep up with the old darling."

"I'm afraid *I* couldn't keep up with her this time." Elizabeth felt absolutely terrible. Mrs. Bramble looked so sweet in her lilac traveling suit, her kindly face turned toward the kitchen, looking for her pet. "Sally was already gone when I got back, Mrs. Bramble. I've asked all the neighbors, but no one has seen her."

For the first time Mrs. Bramble seemed to understand. Her tired eyes filled quickly, and her voice began to tremble. "You mean my Sally's lost? You mean my girl is all alone somewhere?"

Elizabeth wanted to cry herself. The dog was all Mrs. Bramble had in the world.

"You must forgive me, please." Mrs. Bramble was crying freely now, tears streaming down her cheeks. "Ever since my husband died, Sally's been all the family I have." She reached into her purse for a handkerchief and dabbed her eyes. "I know it seems silly to make such a fuss over a dog, but my little girl and I have taken care of each other for such a long time."

Mrs. Wakefield put her arms around Mrs. Bramble and held her without saying a word. Elizabeth knew how helpless her mother felt. After all, no words could bring Sally back.

Suddenly, though, the little woman sat up straight and tall. She forced her voice to stay calm as she decided on a course of action. "Well," she announced, replacing her handkerchief and standing up, "if Sally's lost, we'll just have to find her. She knows my voice. My Sally's old, but she always comes when I call her."

Elizabeth's mother took Mrs. Bramble's arm, and the three of them started out the back door. They showed Mrs. Bramble where Sally had been tied, and then tried to retrace the spaniel's escape route. Even though Amy and Elizabeth had already knocked on every door in the neighborhood, Mrs. Bramble felt sure that Sally was wandering somewhere nearby, lost and confused.

For over half an hour, they walked around the house and up and down the neighboring streets. In her thin, wavering voice, Mrs. Bramble kept calling Sally's name. The sound made Elizabeth's heart break. She would have given anything to see the shaggy old dog step out of the shadows. But there was no sign of Sally anywhere.

The more miserable and tearful Sally's owner became, the more determined Elizabeth and her mother were to find the missing dog. Each time Mrs. Bramble cried out Sally's name, Mrs. Wakefield or Elizabeth would call it again. "Sally!" they yelled across the Welches' backyard. "Sally!" they yelled, as they passed the Pearces' porch. Before long, all three of them were hoarse, and it was too dark to see.

It was no use: Sally was nowhere to be found. Discouraged and more tired than ever, they tramped back to the house with an angry Mrs. Wakefield in their lead. "I want you to call the Fowlers' house," she told Elizabeth as they walked into the kitchen. "Tell Jessica to get her things together right away. We're going over to get her so she can help us look for Sally."

That was just what Elizabeth had been dreading. Jessica wouldn't be back from the concert for at least half an hour. Unless she could think of a way to stall, they would certainly arrive at the Fowlers' before her sister! Even though Elizabeth knew how wrong it had been of Jessica to sneak off to the show, she hated to see her twin's dream concert turn into a nightmare.

"Mom, if we wait to get Jessica, it will be too dark to see anything at all. Just let me find a flashlight, and you and I can take one more walk around the block while Mrs. Bramble rests here with a cup of tea."

"The tea," Mrs. Wakefield told Elizabeth, "is a good idea. But waiting to pick up your sister is *not*. This terrible mess is all Jessica's doing, and she should be here to help get us out of it."

If only Elizabeth could keep them from leaving for another fifteen minutes, it might give Jessica a chance to get back to the Fowlers' in time to meet them. "Maybe," she suggested quickly, "we should call the police before we call Jess. After all, they might have found Sally. Or maybe a neighbor has called them, someone who lives farther away than we walked."

"Do you think so?" Mrs. Bramble looked suddenly hopeful. "Do you suppose someone has already found my Sally?"

Elizabeth went to the phone while her mother poured three cups of hot tea. She dialed the police and gave them a detailed description of Sally, right down to the blue leather collar and her silver dog tag. But the officer who took down the description told her that no one had called about a missing dog at all. He said they would keep the information on file and call Mrs. Bramble as soon as anything turned up.

The call had been too short to give Jessica enough time, and it made things worse than ever. Now Mrs. Bramble was sure that her pet had wandered into some terrible accident. "If someone had found Sally," she told them, pushing away her steaming tea, "they would have called the police. My poor old girl can hardly see."

The color drained from Mrs. Bramble's face as she thought of all the awful things that could have happened to Sally. Mrs. Wakefield, too, looked pale as she watched Sally's owner lose hope. "I'm getting the car keys," she announced, striding purposefully toward the closet. "I'll meet you and Mrs. Bramble out front."

"But wait!" Elizabeth protested. "I haven't even called the Fowlers' yet."

Her mother no longer felt like waiting. "It doesn't matter. We'll just go and pick your sister up."

Things seemed hopeless. If they drove to the Fowlers' now, there was no telling what price Jessica would have to pay for her deception. Elizabeth was desperate for a little more time. "Wait just a minute, could you, Mom. I absolutely *have* to go to the bathroom before we leave."

"Elizabeth Wakefield, if you're not out in front of this house in exactly two minutes, I'm leaving without you!"

Everything was lost. Soon they would be parked in front of the Fowler house, and her mother would hear the horrible truth from the housekeeper. Elizabeth almost wished her mother *would* leave without her. She didn't know whom she felt sorriest for—Mrs. Bramble, who'd lost her beloved pet; Jessica, who was about to be grounded for the rest of her life; or herself, caught yet again in one of her sister's crazy schemes!

Suddenly, as she climbed into the car beside Mrs. Bramble and her mother, Elizabeth got a terrific, brilliant, lifesaving idea! Why hadn't she thought of it sooner?

"Hold everything, Mom," she bubbled excitedly. "I'll bet I know where Sally is!"

"Where, dear?" Mrs. Bramble sounded a little hopeful again.

"Why, home, of course. Don't you see? Maybe Sally got homesick and the first chance she got, she headed for home."

"I'm not sure," said Mrs. Bramble. "I don't think Sally would know how to get home from here. She's never walked that far alone."

"I'm afraid Mrs. Bramble is right, Elizabeth,"

her mother told her. "Perhaps if she were stronger and younger . . ."

"You don't need to be strong to have a nose for home," insisted Elizabeth. "Lots of animals find their way back from much farther away. Remember Lassie?"

"Lassie *did* come home," her mother agreed doubtfully.

"Of course she did," Elizabeth persisted. "And when Sally's after something, there's not a dog in the world with more determination."

"You're right about that," admitted Mrs. Wakefield, remembering the way that Sally had managed to wake Jessica up each morning. "Perhaps it's worth a try."

Mrs. Bramble's expression brightened, and she wiped her eyes. "Do you really think my Sally could travel that far by herself?"

Suddenly Elizabeth wanted it all to be true. Even though she had been stalling, she couldn't bear to build up Mrs. Bramble's hopes, only to have them dashed when they arrived at Shady Dale Court. "I'll bet Sally could run the marathon if she wanted to," she told the dog's owner.

"OK, then," Mrs. Wakefield announced, "we'll stop by Shady Dale Court. It's on the way to the Fowlers' anyway."

Elizabeth could tell that her mother, too, didn't want to build Mrs. Bramble's hopes sky high.

"Great!" Elizabeth was anxious to get to Mrs. Bramble's house, but she hadn't forgotten about her sister. "Just let me go get Sally's leash, so if we

find her we'll be able to hold on to her this time."
She bounded back to the house. Every delay she
created now would give Jessica a few more precious minutes to get back safely to the Fowlers'!

As she picked up the leash, Elizabeth heard
her mother honk the horn impatiently. She raced
back to the waiting car, praying that her plan
would buy enough time to save her adventurous
twin!

Ten

When Elizabeth got back to the car, Mrs. Bramble
insisted on changing seats with her. That way,
Mrs. Bramble could sit by the window and call out
Sally's name as they drove. All the way to Shady
Dale Court, Mrs. Bramble leaned out of the window, straining to find her pet in the dark. Elizabeth, too, peered anxiously into the night. But she
saw nothing except the empty streets and rows of
neatly trimmed lawns. By the time they reached
Mrs. Bramble's house, Elizabeth felt like crying.

They pulled into the driveway without having
seen a trace of the brown spaniel. But Elizabeth
refused to give up hope. She jumped out of the car
and began calling Sally. Mrs. Bramble followed behind her, while Mrs. Wakefield turned on the car's
high beams to light their way across the yard. All
three searched the front and back of the house
with no luck. Soon Elizabeth forgot completely
about stalling for time. The only thing she cared
about now was finding Sally and putting an end
to Mrs. Bramble's unhappiness.

It was no use, though. They didn't see so much as a pawprint, and it was Mrs. Bramble who finally decided they must face facts. "It's just no good, my dears," she told them, tears streaming down her face. "My Sally's gone, and our running around in the dark won't change things." She headed back toward the car, sounding braver and more tired than she had all evening. "Please help me with my suitcase now."

Dejectedly, Elizabeth and her mother gathered Mrs. Bramble's belongings from the car as the old woman unlocked her front door. When Mrs. Bramble turned on the lights, they followed her in and blinked in disbelief. In the middle of the living room, the closest thing to a smile on her furry face, sat Sally!

"Oh!" Mrs. Bramble fell to her knees beside the spaniel. "Oh, Sally! Sally!" She couldn't say anything more before she was smothered with moist kisses. She hugged her pet, rocking back and forth with the shaggy bundle in her arms.

Elizabeth felt a wave of relief and happiness pass over her. She looked at her mother, and they hugged each other excitedly. "Thank goodness!" Mrs. Wakefield declared.

Elizabeth couldn't have been happier if Sally were her own pet. With her arm around her mother, she watched the reunion with delight. But she was very curious, too.

"Mrs. Bramble," Elizabeth said, "I know Sally's a smart dog, but how on earth did she get into this house?"

"Why, my little darling just walked right in

through her dog door." Mrs. Bramble stood up and bustled into the kitchen. "You see, I've had a small door put in beside the kitchen entrance, so she can run in the yard whenever she wants. When you get to be my age, it's not easy to go walking as often as a healthy dog likes!"

Mrs. Wakefield and Elizabeth followed their hostess into the kitchen. Sure enough, a square had been cut into the door at the back of the house. It had its own magnetic flap for a door, and it allowed Sally to go in or out at will.

With the mystery solved, neither Elizabeth nor her mother was anxious to leave this happy scene. Elizabeth begged to help Mrs. Bramble feed Sally, and soon all three were watching the spaniel devour a bowl of her favorite soft chow.

Now that her pet had been found, Mrs. Bramble became her friendly, energetic self. She put a pot of water on the stove and set three plates on the table. "Let's relax and have some tea," she suggested.

Indeed, as they sat talking in the brightly lit kitchen, Elizabeth reflected that nothing had ever tasted as good as the oatmeal squares Mrs. Bramble fished from her cookie jar. Warm and relaxed for the first time that night, none of them had ever had a better reason to celebrate!

At last they had time to catch up on Mrs. Bramble's vacation and Sally's stay at the Wakefields'. While the tired dog snoozed under her mistress's chair, the three chatted like old friends. The minutes passed quickly and pleasantly until Mrs. Wakefield remembered Jessica.

"I'm so glad we got our happy ending," she

told Mrs. Bramble. "But I'm afraid there's still one loose end left to tie up. With your permission, I intend to bring Jessica back here tonight to apologize to you for her carelessness."

"Good heavens," protested Mrs. Bramble. "I certainly don't need any apologies. I have everything I want now that my girl is safe."

"I know you do." Mrs. Wakefield smiled. "But I think it's important that my daughter learn not to take responsibility so lightly. And I'm requesting your help in teaching her a lesson I hope will last."

Mrs. Bramble nodded slowly. "All right," she agreed. "Apologies will be accepted right here just as soon as you pick up your daughter. She's such a charming girl. But I promise I'll try not to let her off too easily!"

As Mrs. Wakefield drove the car up to the Fowlers' driveway, Elizabeth pleaded to be the one to go in and get Jessica. She was sure her sister would rather hear the bad news from someone else before she faced their mother. But the bad news got worse just as Elizabeth stepped out of the car.

"Don't forget," Mrs. Wakefield called after her, "to tell Jessica to bring the money Mrs. Bramble paid her. I want her to return every penny."

"But, Mom . . ."

"But nothing! No daughter of mine is going to accept payment for a job she didn't do. If she doesn't have it with her, we'll drive home to get it. Either way, I expect that money to be returned tonight."

It was a far worse punishment than their

mother knew. Where on earth, Elizabeth wondered, could her twin possibly get twenty-five dollars to repay Mrs. Bramble? The money Jessica earned had already been spent on her ticket for the concert. All the silly excuses Elizabeth had concocted to delay their mother were useless now. Even if Jessica was safely back from the show, she still had some fancy explaining to do. How could she account for the missing money? At that moment, Elizabeth wouldn't have traded places with her twin for anything!

As she rang the Fowlers' door bell, Elizabeth was anxious to bail her sister out of trouble. But when the door opened, she felt more like choking Jessica than helping her. There stood her twin in the elegant marble hall, wearing the brand-new dress Elizabeth had bought for herself for the sixth-grade dance! At first, Elizabeth was so hurt and angry she didn't even notice the large gold hoop hanging from one of Jessica's ears.

"How could you?" Elizabeth stared at the cream-colored dress and the soft leather shoes. "I bought that outfit with my own money. I saved for it the same way I saved for Mom's earrings . . ."

Jessica raised her hands too late to cover the shining hoop. And now, the look of shock that spread across her pretty face matched her twin's. Both girls realized at the same time that Jessica was wearing only *one* of her mother's birthday earrings. The other was missing!

"It must be upstairs. I must have lost it after we came back. Quick, Lizzie! Please, help me look!" Without even asking her sister why she'd come, Jessica turned and bolted up the great circular staircase. Elizabeth raced after her, and soon the two were on their hands and knees, searching every inch of Lila Fowler's bedroom rug.

Lila joined them, and all three searched together for as long as Elizabeth dared to keep her mother waiting in the car outside. "It's no use," she announced finally. "It's just not here. You must have lost it at the concert." She stood up and nodded toward the stairs. "And if you think *this* is trouble, you should see what's waiting for you outside!"

Quickly, as Jessica gathered her clothes together and stuffed them into her overnight bag, Elizabeth explained the situation. "You're lucky, Jess," she told her twin. "Things would have been a lot worse if we hadn't found Sally. But Mom is still fuming, and she wants you to apologize to Mrs. Bramble tonight."

"Liz?" Jessica looked at her sister timidly. "You didn't tell her, did you? I mean, you didn't mention the concert?" Jessica was beginning to wish she'd never heard of Johnny Buck.

"Of course not. Right now, Jessica Wakefield, I think you're about the lowest, sneakiest sister anybody could ever have. Still, I know you wouldn't tell on *me* if *I* pulled a dumb stunt like this." She braced one knee on the bulging bag and helped Jessica zip it closed. "Besides, why should I make Mom feel worse than she already does?"

"You're terrific, Liz. And don't worry, I'll make everything up to you. I promise." For once, Jessica sounded as if she really meant it.

The twins waved a quick goodbye to Lila, then hurried downstairs. At the door, Elizabeth stopped suddenly, realizing she'd forgotten to break the worst news of all. "You may be able to make everything up to me," she told her sister. "But Mom wants you to make everything up to Mrs. Bramble, too!"

"What do you mean?"

"I mean she wants you to give Mrs. Bramble her money back. Right now. Tonight."

"But I can't!" wailed Jessica.

"I know that, Jess. And you know that. But you're going to have a hard time explaining it to Mom." Elizabeth opened the door, and they both saw their mother's headlights cutting across the darkness.

"Liz," Jessica whispered as they walked toward the car. "Don't you have some money you could lend me?"

"You know I don't," Elizabeth whispered back. "You're wearing the last money I had in the world on your left ear!"

Jessica slid miserably into the seat beside her mother, prepared for the worst. "Mom," she began, "Elizabeth told me about Sally. I'm so sorry, really I am. I wouldn't hurt Mrs. Bramble for anything."

"You hurt her for a night at Lila's. I'm really disappointed in you, Jessica."

Jessica thought that the worst thing about being reprimanded by her mother wasn't usually the punishment itself. It was the awful way Jessica felt about herself for letting her mother down. Jessica's eyes began to fill with tears.

Mrs. Wakefield pulled out of the driveway and drove in silence toward Mrs. Bramble's house. When they came to the first stop sign, she turned to Jessica. "I was so proud of you for taking this job, honey. It meant facing something you'd always been afraid of. But unfortunately, instead of facing it, you ran away. I know Steven and Elizabeth spent more time taking care of Sally than you did."

Jessica was too ashamed to argue. When they edged into Mrs. Bramble's driveway, Jessica was in no hurry to get out of the car. She had no idea what she was going to say to the elderly woman. She would rather stay in the car, listening to her mother's lecture, than face someone she'd almost hurt past fixing. How could she ever explain?

"I don't know what you're going to tell her, young lady." Her mother seemed to have read Jessica's thoughts. "But I want you to make it clear that you're sorry you put fun ahead of your job. Mrs. Bramble doesn't have scores of friends like you. She doesn't have a family. All she has is the dog you nearly lost for good."

"I know, Mom." Jessica felt the tears start again. There were hundreds of souvenir caps, but only one Sally.

"Jessica." She felt her mother's gentle touch on her shoulder. "You didn't do anything deliberately. I understand that. And I'm sure Mrs. Bramble will understand, too."

Slowly Jessica climbed out of the car and walked toward the house. She saw Mrs. Bramble's kitchen light shining and watched the woman's shadow cross in front of the window. If only Elizabeth could come with her! Her twin always knew just the right thing to say. But this time, Jessica knew, she couldn't lean on her sister. She took the single gold earring off her ear and slipped it into the dress pocket. Then she pushed the door bell and listened to it ring inside. The door opened. Jessica took a deep breath and walked in to face Mrs. Bramble alone.

Eleven

◇

Jessica had stepped into the same friendly, comfortable living room where she had first met Sally. But this visit felt very different. Mrs. Bramble's kindly face looked tired, and the cheerful smile Jessica remembered had been replaced by an anxious frown. There was one thing, though, that was still the same. Peering underneath the blue couch, Jessica found the old spaniel in her favorite spot, snoozing in perfect contentment. How happy she was to see that silly dog again!

"I'm so glad you found Sally, Mrs. Bramble," Jessica began. "And I'm sorry as I can be that I lost her." Tears were beginning to shine in her aqua eyes.

"I know you're sorry, my dear," Mrs. Bramble began. "And I'm sure the next time you're caring for someone smaller and more helpless than you are, you won't forget the lesson you learned today."

Jessica sank into the plump sofa cushion, wishing she could disappear. Mrs. Bramble had the same quiet way of scolding that her mother did. She hated to think that this gentle woman would probably never trust her again!

"You know, Jessica," Mrs. Bramble continued, "Sally took good care of me at a time in my life when I needed affection and friendship." The slender woman looked fondly at the two furry, brown paws poking out from under the sofa. "Now that she's old, I have to take care of her."

"I—I never thought of Sally as old." Jessica remembered the lightning flash that had streaked after the Blaneys' cat. "I guess I didn't think about anyone but myself."

"Well, fortunately your mistake didn't cost Sally her life or me my most precious old friend. But I hope you understand that it might have."

"I do, Mrs. Bramble." Jessica felt very small and very foolish. There was a huge lump in her throat, and her voice sounded all wobbly and soft. "My mom wants me to give you back the money you paid me. And she's right. I really didn't earn it. I only wish I *could* pay you back, but I can't. I . . ."

"I know you can't return the money, dear." Mrs. Bramble smiled at Jessica. "You've already spent it on your mother's present."

"Well, I *did* need the money right away." Jessica felt worse than ever, recalling the way she had let the old woman think she was spending the twenty-five dollars for her mother's birthday.

"You certainly were in a hurry," agreed Mrs. Bramble. "I'll bet you bought something really special for your mother. Even though your brain was careless, your heart was certainly in the right place."

"No, it wasn't." Jessica surprised herself by interrupting Mrs. Bramble in a firm, clear voice. "My heart wasn't in the right place at all!"

"Why, what do you mean, child?"

"I mean I've been a horrible, awful cheat, and I wish I could drop right through this floor!" Suddenly Jessica wanted to tell Mrs. Bramble everything, even if she could never face her parents with the whole story. She desperately needed to get it out into the open now.

"I never meant to hurt anyone. I—I just wanted to hear 'Saturday Blues' and see The Buck."

"The Buck?" Mrs. Bramble looked confused.

"Yes. He's a rock-music star, Mrs. Bramble. And he played right here in Sweet Valley this afternoon."

Jessica told Mrs. Bramble the whole story. How she had waited an entire year to see her singing idol. How every kid in town had been looking forward to the concert. And how her parents had flatly refused to let her go.

"You mean you went to the show today against your parents' orders?"

"Yes. And I never bought my mother a present either. I spent the money on my ticket to the show. I took my sister's best dress without asking. I lost my mother's earrings. And I was the world's worst dog-sitter ever. I let my sister walk Sally because I'm scared to death of dogs."

Jessica was sobbing into her hands, her shoulders hunched and her whole body shaking. Mrs. Bramble sat beside her, stroking Jessica's blond hair and soothing her as best she could.

"There, there, dear. I don't know anything about blue Saturdays, but I know lots about young girls. I know one in particular who dyed her hair bright red, even after her mother strictly forbade her."

"You do?" Jessica stopped sobbing and opened her eyes.

"Yes. I know her very well. And I can tell you that her mischievous beginnings didn't prevent her from growing up to be a fairly respectable woman." Mrs. Bramble was smiling at Jessica with twinkling eyes. "Even if I say so myself."

"You mean . . . ?"

"That's right. *I* sneaked off to a friend's house when I was just about your age. Then, my friend and I did two of the most unspeakable things."

"You did?" Jessica's eyes were red but curious.

"We certainly did. We hennaed our hair, and we pierced our ears. When I came home, my mother took one look at me and burst into tears!"

Jessica smiled gratefully. Then a small frown formed as she thought about her own parents and how wrong she'd been to disobey them. "Did you get punished?"

"I certainly did." Mrs. Bramble popped into the kitchen and returned with a plate of oatmeal squares. "I was not allowed to visit my friend for a month and, worst of all, I had to live with that horrible red hair until it all grew out!"

They laughed, and Jessica felt better as she bit into one of the cookies. "I'm glad I don't have to do anything like that," she said. "But I still don't know how I can ever face my parents."

"I think you'll have no trouble so long as you know you're paying for what you did."

"But I just told you, Mrs. Bramble. I can't give you back the money."

"Maybe not. But you *can* work it off. Jessica, I'm going to tell your mother that I refused to take back the money, but that I accepted your kind offer to walk Sally every day for the next month."

"Month?"

"That's how long it's going to take for my niece to move here from Maryland. My arthritis is getting worse, and she'll be able to help me get around a little better. Meanwhile you can make sure Sally gets the exercise *she* needs. It's a perfect solution, don't you think?"

"A whole month?"

"Every morning before school, and every afternoon before dinner."

"Saturdays, too?"

"Even Sundays."

Jessica looked down at her feet. She could hear Sally snoring comfortably under the sofa. A whole month of tugging that fat bundle of energy around on a leash! A whole month of stopping every few feet while everyone in the world patted the "cute doggie." A month of absolute, complete torture.

"I guess it's only fair," she said, smiling at last.

*   *   *

By the time Jessica, Elizabeth, and their mother got back to the house, Steven had returned from the concert and was busy raiding the refrigerator.

"I don't understand why you haven't exploded long ago," Jessica commented, walking into the kitchen. She felt deliciously relieved to be with her family—even with Steven. She hugged her brother and stole a pickle from the heap of food he'd plundered from the refrigerator.

"I saw that, Jess," he told her. "Your hand is definitely not quicker than my eye."

"That's OK," Jessica replied. "I'm in a fabulous mood, so you can tease me as much as you want."

Steven was mystified. "What's wrong with *her*?" he asked his mother and Elizabeth, who soon joined them at the table for a late-night snack. "I thought she'd be mad at the world after missing The Buck."

"Well, I should be," Jessica told her brother. "But I bet after you've told us all about the show, I'll feel as if I'd been there myself." She glanced quickly at Elizabeth, who looked as if she could hardly keep from laughing. Jessica flashed her a big grin. As long as she could make her twin smile, she knew everything would be fine.

And it was. As soon as they had finished their snack, the girls raced upstairs to Elizabeth's room. Jessica couldn't wait to set things straight with her sister. She owed her an apology, and she had a special present to give her. Unzipping her overnight bag, Jessica pulled out the striped cap from Johnny Buck.

"I didn't get it autographed, and I didn't even get a chance to talk to Johnny. But I did figure out who should have this cap in her bedroom." She handed Elizabeth the hat and hugged her with all the love she felt.

"Lizzie, I am the sorriest excuse for a twin in the world. Can you ever forgive me?"

"Only if you get out of my dress this instant and promise to wash and iron it before the dance!" Elizabeth smiled. "And by the way, Jess, I have a present for *you*—or Mrs. Bramble does. She asked me to give this to you." Elizabeth handed her sister the small package Mrs. Bramble had left with her earlier that evening. "Go on," she coaxed. "I'm sure she still wants you to have it."

Slowly Jessica unwrapped the gift. As soon as she had opened the small box, she passed it to Elizabeth. "Here," she told her sister. "It doesn't begin to make up for the beautiful earrings you bought, but I think it will make a terrific birthday present for Mom. Don't you?"

Elizabeth looked inside the box. There, nestled in soft cotton, was a bracelet. It was formed by six slender black and silver bands held together with a silver catch. It was one of the prettiest pieces of jewelry Elizabeth had ever seen.

"And I want *you* to give it to her." Jessica stole a longing glance at the pretty bracelet. She would have loved to have kept it for herself, but her mother and sister meant more to her than any bracelet anywhere. She was sure Mrs. Bramble would understand.

Now it was Elizabeth's turn to hug Jessica. "It will be from *both* of us," she assured her twin gratefully. Then, her arm still around her sister, she caught sight of the two of them in the mirror on the bathroom door. "Look at us," she giggled. "A real study in opposites."

Jessica looked into the glass. There she saw the reflections of two blond, turquoise-eyed girls, absolutely identical. The only difference between them was that she wore a smart pale beige dress while Elizabeth sported jeans and a pullover. Her sister's hair had been pulled back into a casual fluff with two brightly colored barrettes. Jessica, on the other hand, had worn her shoulder-length hair loose and flowing.

"You're right," she told her sister solemnly. "We may look like twins, but we are really different. But don't worry, Liz. I'm going to try to be just like you from now on. I'm going to be honest and fair and good as gold. You'll see."

Elizabeth groaned. "Yuck! You make me sound like a total loser, Jess! Besides, if you stopped being so wild, we'd never have any fun."

"But we'd sure have a lot less trouble." Jessica was serious. "I mean it, Liz. I'm going to be so responsible and caring and good, no one will recognize me. Tomorrow morning, first thing, I'm going straight to Mrs. Bramble's and . . ." She stopped in midsentence with a look of horror on her face. "Oh, no!"

"What's the trouble?" Elizabeth was worried by her sister's sudden change of mood.

"It's just that I promised Mrs. Bramble I'd walk Sally tomorrow."

"So?"

"So, I've got this absolutely top-secret, really important meeting of the Unicorns tomorrow morning." Jessica now looked forlorn and confused. "Oh, Liz, do you think you could help me just this once? You know Mrs. Bramble can't tell us apart. If you walk Sally tomorrow, I'll never ask you again. I promise. Cross my heart."

Elizabeth burst out laughing. Then she amazed Jessica by smiling with relief. "Thank goodness," she said, beaming broadly.

"What are you so happy about?" said a perplexed Jessica. "I just begged for another favor."

"I know," answered Elizabeth. "And I'm certainly *not* going to do it for you. You're going to have to walk Sally yourself from now on—just like you promised. And you'll have to carry all of Sally's things back to Mrs. Bramble's by yourself, too." She was smiling at her sister, even though she clearly meant what she said. "It's just that for a minute there you sounded like you were really changing. But now I know I've still got my sneaky, crazy sister. And you know what? I think I'll keep her!"

Jessica hugged her twin, then slipped out of Elizabeth's dress and put it in the laundry hamper. "Well, I hope you never change your mind, Liz. If I had to pick one person in the whole, entire universe to be my sister, it would be you. And," she added, remembering her walk with Sally, "if I had to pick one person I *didn't* want, even as a distant relative, it would be our new neighbor."

"What new neighbor?"

"Brooke Dennis. Her family's moved into the

Logginses' house. I've already given her a nickname—'Disgusting Dennis'!"

"I think I met her, and I'm afraid that name fits." Elizabeth recalled the sharp-tongued girl who'd opened the door when she was looking for Sally.

"That's what *everyone's* going to be calling her once she's in school here. As soon as she starts classes at Sweet Valley, look out! If she could kick a dog like Sally, goodness knows how she'll behave around people!"

"She kicked Sally?"

"And the poor old thing wasn't doing anything but licking her. Even your nasty little sister wouldn't stoop *that* low!"

"Well," agreed Elizabeth, "anyone who could hurt our old Sally sure isn't winning any popularity votes with me. But let's give her a chance, Jess." Elizabeth knew how quickly her sister formed opinions of people and how wrong she'd been about some of them—like Amy Sutton. "After all, how would you feel coming to a new school in the middle of the year?"

"Not half as bad as Miss Uppity's going to feel." Jessica collapsed onto Elizabeth's bed, scheming already. "That is if *I* have anything to say about it!"

Jessica's not the only one with plans for Brooke Dennis. Be sure to read **The New Girl, Sweet Valley Twins #6.**